THE PHANTOM MUSIC BOX

THE HAUNTED MUSEUM

THE PHANTOM MUSIC BOX

BOOK TWO

Suzanne Weyn

SCHOLASTIC INC.

No part of this publication may be reproduced, stored in a retrieval system, or transmitted in any form or by any means, electronic, mechanical, photocopying, recording, or otherwise, without written permission of the publisher. For information regarding permission, write to Scholastic Inc., Attention: Permissions Department, 557 Broadway, New York, NY 10012.

ISBN 978-0-545-58845-4

12 11 10 9 8 7 6 5 4 3 2 1   14 15 16 17 18 19/0

Printed in the U.S.A.   40
First printing, February 2014

The text type was set in Old Style 7.
Book design by Abby Kuperstock

To Bill Gonzalez. XXOO. And thanks.

INTRODUCTION

You have arrived at the Haunted Museum. It's a place where dreams are made — bad dreams! Ghostly phantasms float by. When you least expect it, a hand grabs your throat. A jar falls and unleashes an ancient curse. An old-fashioned music box plays a tune you'd rather forget.

I opened the Haunted Museum many, *many* years ago. And I've been adding to its "special" displays for longer than even I can recall.

Some say the museum has become a worldwide chain — just an entertaining fraud for the amusement of tourists.

Others see something more mysterious, more sinister, within its walls.

Either way, no one escapes unaffected by what they find within the museum. The items that touch your hands will come back to touch your life in a most terrifying manner.

Take, for instance, the case of Emma Bryant, who is about to dance to the tune of an antique music box she defiantly touches: a music box of death!

Da-da-da-da DUM Dee-dum dee-dum Da-da-da-da DUM Dee-dum dee-dum

Happy Haunting,

Belladonna Bloodstone

Founder and Head Curator

THE HAUNTED MUSEUM

Twelve-year-old Emma Bryant knew she should be in her ballet/modern dance class rather than here in the Haunted Museum. Not that the other students would miss her — those perfect girls with their perfect dancing form.

Emma recalled her last dance class and cringed. During her attempt to plié, she'd crashed into Elizabeth McGowen, the best dancer in class. Knocking Elizabeth back had resulted in the entire group behind their star dancer toppling over. Emma knew her face had blazed red under the angry looks the other girls had cast her way as they helped one another up.

No, taking off from dance class was not what she should have been doing right now. Emma figured she needed all the practice she could get.

But this trip to the Haunted Museum was how her best friend, Keera Kramer, wanted to spend her twelfth birthday, so how could she not go?

Keera had been waiting to visit the Haunted Museum since the girls had been in the second grade. Her parents had said it was too frightening, but they'd finally relented and were allowing Keera to hold her party there.

"Man, they *really* don't want you to touch their stuff, do they?" Keera leaned in close to Emma to comment. DO NOT TOUCH signs were hanging everywhere.

"It makes me want to touch something just to see what would happen," Emma said with a grin.

"Don't do it!" Keera warned. "My parents would freak if we set off all the alarms in the Haunted Museum." They both glanced across the room at Mr. and Mrs. Kramer, who were looking at an exhibit called Bizarre Oddities, which featured shrunken heads, a bat with an eerily human face, a two-headed cow, and that sort of thing. The girls' friends Lauren and Stella had already made their way over to a special Haunted Music Boxes exhibit and were nearly out of sight.

Emma had never been in a Haunted Museum before. But so far it seemed like a sort of cross between Madame Tussauds wax museum, Ripley's Believe It or Not!, and The Haunted Mansion in Walt Disney World. In the front chambers of the place were a motion-activated talking skeleton dressed to be Long John Silver, the pirate; a shredded mummy who jolted into a sitting position from his coffin; and the body of the space alien they claimed crashed in Roswell, New Mexico, back in 1947.

Emma stopped to examine the crinkly, grayish figure lying on a plank. Its eyes were closed but the large eyeballs bulged beneath its lids. Was it real? It was hard to tell.

"It's fake," Emma decided.

"It looks pretty real to me," Keera disagreed.

"How would this place get a real alien?" Emma asked. "Don't you think the space program or the government or someone would have it?"

"I suppose," Keera said. Still, it did seem pretty convincing. Even Emma bent to examine it more closely.

"Don't touch!" a guard barked harshly as she pointed to one of several DO NOT TOUCH signs on the walls.

Emma jumped back, her hands in the air. "I wasn't going to!"

The guard glowered at her. "See that you don't!"

"Wow! What's bugging *her*?" Emma griped once the guard moved away.

"They really, *really* don't want you touching things," Keera said in a low tone. She tugged Emma's sleeve. "Everyone's already gone into the Haunted Music Boxes exhibit — come on!"

The tinkling of spooky music played softly as Emma and Keera crossed into a shadowy, narrow room. Mirrors on the walls gave Emma the feeling of being in a maze. She caught sight of Lauren and Stella studying a music box and then realized that there seemed to be ten of them. Their reflections were bouncing off the many mirrors. The music boxes sat with their lids open on shelves lit from above. The first one was a porcelain skull. The top of its head was flipped up to show sculpted worms, while a recording of screams played. "That's so gross!" Keera said, impressed.

The next music box was in the shape of a haunted house. Every two minutes, the door swung open to unleash maniacal cackling from within. *That's not scary,* Emma decided.

The next music box played a French tune as a small guillotine inside dropped on the head of a tiny doll lying under its blade. The head bobbed on a spring before popping back in place on the doll's neck so the blade could fall on it all over again. "That's kind of cool," Emma said.

"It's creepy," Keera said with a shiver.

Emma wasn't especially frightened by the exhibit, though she did find the music boxes intriguing. It was such a change from the usual sweetness of music boxes, and she loved all the intricate details. "There are some bizarre minds out there," she remarked to Keera.

"Yeah. Tell me about it," Keera agreed.

Near the end of the exhibit hall, Emma saw a doorway into the gift shop. Stella and Lauren were already in there with Keera's parents.

"We'd better hurry and meet everyone in the gift shop. They're probably waiting for us so we can go have lunch," Keera said.

Emma heard Keera speaking, but she wasn't really paying attention. Instead, she drifted over to a smaller display case. Emma inspected a highly polished wooden music box whose cover had been lifted to show a lovely scene of a man and woman dancing a ballet.

The little male doll in the box wore a velvet coat and dancing tights. His feet were turned out and his arms were held in front of his body.

The woman doll's curls were piled on top of her head and she was dressed in a dance costume of velvet and pink tulle netting. She stood high on pointe shoes, her arms in a circle over her head.

A hauntingly melodic piece of music played gently as the figures turned in circles. *Da-da-da-da DUM Dee-dum dee-dum Da-da-da-da DUM Dee-dum dee-dum*

"That's pretty," Keera remarked. "And look, the scene is reflected in the mirror on the inside of the cover." A wide oval mirror sat in the middle of a satin cloth.

"Why would something this pretty be in a haunted music box exhibition?" Emma wondered. She leaned closer to get a better look at the twirling couple.

"I've warned you already! Haven't I?"

Emma looked up into the red face of the same scowling guard who'd scolded them earlier. "Do not touch!" she snarled.

"I didn't even lay a finger on the stupid —"

Keera grabbed Emma's arm. "We were just leaving," she told the guard with forced cheer, pulling Emma toward the gift shop.

With a disapproving grunt, the guard walked back toward the doorway to the rest of the museum.

"What a crab," Emma grumbled.

"Forget about her," Keera advised, still pulling Emma along. They were about to step into the gift shop when Emma broke loose of Keera's grip.

"What are you —?" she heard Keera mumble as she hurried back to the music box with the dancing couple.

Emma knew she was being childish, but she couldn't help herself. The guard had made her angry. She acted as if it would be the end of the world if Emma touched something when she'd never intended to!

Her eyes flashing defiantly, Emma pressed her thumb on the mirror until she left an unmistakable print. "How do you like that?!" she whispered at the guard, who stood looking away at the other end of the hall.

A shiver swept down Emma's spine, but she decided to ignore it. It felt good to do things her way for once.

Keera was instantly at her side, clutching her arm. "You're going to get us kicked out," she complained.

"Calm down. I didn't hurt anything," Emma assured her, and they hurried into the gift shop.

2

AT HOME that night over dinner, Emma told her parents about the Haunted Museum, sparing no detail of the two-headed cow, cursed necklaces, and alien body they'd seen.

"It sounds grotesque," Mrs. Bryant remarked, and speared a bite of cauliflower with her fork.

"It sounds *cool* to me," her nine-year-old brother, Jason, disagreed. "I wish I could've gone."

"I can think of many more useful ways to spend one's time than immersing oneself in the macabre, can't you?" Mr. Bryant commented as he cleaned his glasses with his napkin.

Emma turned to her mother. "What did he say?" Mr. Bryant was a middle school English teacher and believed in speaking well.

"Dad, why can't you just speak regular English?" Jason added.

Mr. Bryant just sighed and returned to his meal.

"Your father doesn't see the point in spending time on spooky, bizarre subjects," Mrs. Bryant explained.

"Oh," Emma said.

"Ellen, I can speak for myself," Mr. Bryant complained to his wife. "But, yes, that's what I meant."

The doorbell rang and Jason ran to answer it.

"Who is it?" Mrs. Bryant called.

In a few moments, the door closed and Jason returned holding a cardboard carton. "No one was there, but this box was sitting on the doorstep. It's from the Haunted Museum, for Emma."

"It must be a party favor from the Kramers," Mrs. Bryant said. "How kind of them. Open it, Emma."

Emma jabbed at the tape with her supper knife until the box was open. Inside was a gleaming wooden music box. It was just like the one she'd left her thumbprint on. Emma's heart raced. Who had sent this? Why?

"How lovely!" Mrs. Bryant said with enthusiasm. "Is it a replica of something you saw in the museum?"

"It hardly deserves to be called a museum, dear," Mr. Bryant objected.

"You know what I mean," Mrs. Bryant said.

"There was a Haunted Music Boxes exhibit,"

Emma told them, still staring down at the music box.

"That's dumb!" Jason declared. "It's not even scary."

"No doubt it's the only item from the gift shop that the Kramers deemed suitable," Mr. Bryant decided.

"They're no fun," Jason grumbled. "They should have sent something cool."

"Let's see it, Emma," Mrs. Bryant urged.

Emma lifted out the music box just as Mrs. Bryant's cell phone rang. "It's your dance school," she said, checking the caller ID. "They probably want to know where you were today."

The Bryants had a family rule about not answering cell phones during supper, but Mrs. Bryant must have felt the meal was already disrupted because she took the call, wandering into the kitchen as she spoke to the person on the other end of the phone.

Emma returned the music box to its cardboard carton and set it aside. Mrs. Bryant was smiling when she returned from the kitchen. "That was Madame Andrews from the dance school."

"Hoping I'd fallen off a cliff and was never coming back?" Emma asked sarcastically.

"No! Why would you say that?" Mrs. Bryant asked, shocked.

"Because then she wouldn't have to invite me to try out for the dance team."

"Well, that's exactly what she *did* call about," Mrs. Bryant said as she resumed her seat at the dinner table. "She wanted to remind me that I have to sign a permission slip for you to audition for the dance team. Why do you think she doesn't want you to try out?"

"Because I'm the worst one in class," Emma replied.

"Not at all," Mrs. Bryant disagreed. "She just told me you're a very spirited dancer."

"Spirited! That's funny," Emma said. Spirited was one way of putting it. It was better than saying *always one step behind the other dancers*, or *constantly going the wrong way*. Emma loved to dance; she lived for it. And she knew she could be pretty good, too. It was dancing with others that threw her. She just couldn't stay in step.

"Madame Andrews doesn't want me on the dance team and neither do the other girls," Emma said.

"That's nonsense. Why would she request that you audition if she didn't want you?" Mr. Bryant questioned.

"She asks everybody to audition," Emma

explained. "She has to. Madame Andrews wants to seem fair, but I already know I won't make it."

"I think you're a lovely dancer," Mrs. Bryant said.

"That's because you're my mother," Emma replied. "I'm always bumping into someone or something. Two days ago I tripped a girl."

Jason laughed uproariously, but his parents silenced him with withering stares.

"It's true," Emma insisted glumly. "Elizabeth is one of the best dancers in the class, and she was really mad." She'd shouted at Emma for being so clumsy while the others looked on disapprovingly. It had been mortifying.

Emma rubbed her belly unhappily. Just remembering it made her stomach ache. "Can I go to my room?" she asked. "I don't feel so well."

"Of course, dear."

Emma took her music box in its cardboard carton and carried it upstairs to her room.

Inside, Emma sat on her bed with the music box at her side. Pulling her cell phone from her pocket, she sent a text message to her friend. *Thanks for the music box.* ☺

Keera's response came right away. *What?*

The Haunted Museum sent a music box — from you, right?

No idea what you mean, Keera texted.

OK . . . weird. TTYL. Emma signed off.

Emma set her phone aside and pulled the music box onto her lap. If this music box was a copy of the original, it was a very authentic-looking imitation. It had the same highly polished top. The lining and the oval mirror were the same, too. The little figures were identical to the ones she'd seen at the Haunted Museum. They stood in place, poised to begin spinning when the music started.

Peering more closely into the box, Emma gasped.

The thumbprint she'd left on the mirror was right there!

Emma backed away from the music box. "That's impossible!" she cried.

Mrs. Bryant came to the door with a pink bottle of medicine. "What's impossible?" she asked.

"This isn't a copy of the music box in the museum, Mom. It's the *exact* one I saw there."

"Why would they send away a part of their exhibit?" Mrs. Bryant asked as she opened the bottle. "It couldn't be."

"No, it *is*," Emma insisted.

"What makes you think so?"

Emma wasn't sure she wanted to reveal to her mother that she'd left her fingerprint on the mirror after being told repeatedly not to touch anything. "It just looks so *exactly* like it," she said instead. "I mean . . . every tiny detail is the same. Completely the same. It's crazy!"

"That's *good*, isn't it?" Mrs. Bryant said, offering Emma a spoonful of the pink medicine. She checked her daughter's temperature with the back of her palm on Emma's forehead. "Isn't it meant to look like the original?"

"I suppose so."

"Then what's wrong with it being the same?"

Emma sighed. She'd have to confess. "I touched the mirror and left a fingerprint on it. The fingerprint is right there. Look!"

Mrs. Bryant smoothed Emma's hair and

grinned. "Oh, you're being so silly, Emma. Anyone could have touched this and left a print. You might have done it yourself just now. I wouldn't let it concern you."

Scowling at the music box, Emma nodded. Her mother's words made sense, she knew. But still . . .

"There now, get some rest." Mrs. Bryant picked up the music box and examined it. "It's so lovely," she remarked. "Should I play it?"

"No. Later," Emma replied. "I think I *would* like to get some sleep."

"Good idea," Mrs. Bryant agreed, setting the music box on Emma's nightstand. "Take it easy tomorrow so you feel better before school on Monday." She kissed Emma on the forehead and left the room.

Emma changed into her nightgown and climbed under the covers. It was a little early to go to sleep, but it had been a long day and she was tired.

Almost without thinking, Emma took the music box from the nightstand and gazed at the fingerprint on the mirror. Curious, she placed her thumb over it.

The size matched perfectly, but maybe Emma's mom was right. Any number of people could have touched it while the music box was in the gift shop. She couldn't recall *exactly* where she'd touched it, anyway.

Unable to resist hearing a little of the music, Emma wound the small key at the side of the music box.

Da-da-da-da DUM Dee-dum dee-dum Da-da-da-da DUM Dee-dum dee-dum

She recognized the tune right away: "The Blue Danube." Emma checked an app on her phone, which told her it had been written by Johann Strauss in 1867.

The little dancers turned slowly to the tempo of the music, their dance reflected in the oval mirror. It was a cute little music box, she decided. She was just being silly.

Shutting the lid stopped the music. Emma snapped off the light and rolled over, falling into a deep sleep.

• • •

After several hours, Emma gradually came awake. The soft tinkling of "The Blue Danube" was playing in her room. *Da-da-da-da DUM Dee-dum dee-dum Da-da-da-da DUM Dee-dum dee-dum*

Moonlight shone on the music box on her nightstand, and Emma leaned toward it. She was certain she'd shut the lid before falling asleep, but it was open now. The little dancers were moving. . . .

But they were spinning much too fast!

The little dancers whirled at a tremendous speed as the tempo of "The Blue Danube" grew faster and faster, and the music swelled louder, as if an orchestra was playing and not just the tinny music box.

What was happening?

Swinging her legs over the side of the bed, Emma peered into the moonlit music box and reached out to close the lid.

And then she noticed a movement in the oval mirror.

Two eyes were gazing back at her — but the eyes were blue, not brown, like her own.

Emma slammed the lid shut, cutting off the music. Her heart pounded. Someone had been looking at her from the other side of the mirror!

Her school backpack was in a corner of her room. Keeping a firm pressure on the music box lid, Emma used her free hand to spill the backpack's contents onto the floor. Then she stuffed the music box inside and zipped the pack.

For extra security, Emma stuffed the backpack into her dresser drawer and shut it tight.

In the morning, she'd throw the thing in the garbage.

No!

She'd never be able to sleep with the music box in the room. She'd get rid of it right away.

Wrapping herself in the quilt on her bed, Emma took the backpack with the music box out of the drawer and hurried downstairs. In the family room, her parents were watching the news on TV.

She dashed past the doorway, hoping they wouldn't notice her. Emma worried that if she told them what she'd seen, they'd laugh at her, or worse, worry. The last thing she wanted was for them to try to persuade her to keep the music box.

Emma slipped into the kitchen and eased open the back door. She stepped out into the yard and hopped as the cold ground chilled her toes. Shivering, she quickly unzipped her backpack and pulled the top off one of the garbage cans lined up by the side fence. "Out you go," she said as she dumped the music box out of the backpack and replaced the can's lid in a flash.

Crossing her arms for warmth, she ran back to the house. Just as she stepped into the kitchen, a tinkling song caught her attention.

The haunting melody of "The Blue Danube" played from inside the garbage can.

For a moment, Emma froze in place, listening.

Should she go back to shut it off?

No. The image of those strange eyes peering at her from the box came into her mind. There was no way she would take a chance on seeing them again. Closing the door firmly behind her, she hurried upstairs to her room.

In the morning, the sanitation workers would take the eerie music box away — for good.

Emma? Emma!"

Blinking in the morning light, Emma was confused. Why was she on the living room couch, and why was her mother calling to her from her bedroom upstairs?

"Emma! Where are you?"

Then she remembered everything that had happened the night before and went to the bottom of the stairs. "I'm down here, Mom," she called.

Mrs. Bryant appeared at the top of the stairs.

"I couldn't sleep so I came down and slept on the couch," Emma explained. When she'd gone back to her bedroom after throwing out the music box, she'd tried to fall back to sleep but kept waking up. The music box had scared her so much that she didn't even want to be alone in her room. She'd come down to watch TV and fallen asleep on the couch.

Besides, she wanted to know the moment the sanitation truck took the garbage cans away. She'd hear the truck better from the living room. And she had, in fact, heard them very early that morning.

What a relief! The music box was gone.

"Are you all right?" Mrs. Bryant asked.

"Not really," Emma said as she climbed the stairs. "You won't *believe* how weird that music box is." Now that the music box was gone, she could tell her mother about what had happened.

"I can't *believe* what a wreck your room is," her mother countered, heading into Emma's bedroom. "What went on in here?"

Emma followed her in and saw her mother's point. The books, papers, pens, and pencils she'd dumped from her backpack were scattered all over her room, as were the clothes she'd thrown from her dresser drawer to make room for the backpack holding the music box.

"And where is your quilt?" Mrs. Bryant asked.

"On the couch," Emma replied. "The music box was acting really bizarre last night and I had to put it in my backpack and then in the dresser. And then I got so creeped out that I couldn't take it anymore so I —"

"Well, it seems just fine now," Mrs. Bryant cut in.

"Huh?" Emma didn't understand.

Mrs. Bryant gestured at the music box that sat open on Emma's nightstand.

"No way!" How had that gotten there? "I threw that thing away last night."

"Maybe you meant to throw it away, but clearly you didn't," Mrs. Bryant said.

"I'm not imagining it, Mom! I threw this in the garbage can last night."

"Why would you do that?"

"I *told* you! Something's not right with it. I definitely threw it away."

"You weren't feeling well last night, dear. You probably just dreamed you threw it away."

"Ugh," Emma murmured, picking up the music box. *Could* she have dreamed it?

The little dancers seemed back to normal. They stood there looking innocent. The only mark on the oval mirror was the thumbprint. Emma took a tissue from the cardboard box on her dresser and wiped it away.

"You said the box was acting strangely? What exactly was it doing last night?" Mrs. Bryant asked.

Emma told her about the lid opening and the music playing faster and faster, but she felt increasingly foolish as she spoke. Her story was so crazy. She couldn't blame her mother for the skeptical expression that had formed on her face.

"You were *definitely* dreaming," Mrs. Bryant said. "Your father was right about that Haunted Museum. It gave you nightmares."

Mrs. Bryant took the music box from Emma and turned its key until "The Blue Danube" played. *Da-da-da-da DUM Dee-dum dee-dum Da-da-da-da DUM Dee-dum dee-dum*

She hummed along, swaying gently with the

melody. "I adore this piece of music," she remarked. "It's so lovely."

That had to be it, Emma thought. She'd fallen asleep and had had a bad dream. The little figures whirling to a frantic version of "The Blue Danube," the peering eyes — they were only a creepy part of her dream. The music box was perfectly fine now.

But if that was so, she'd also thrown all this stuff around her room.

Emma looked down and realized that her feet were filthy. She'd definitely been outside last night. Had she sleepwalked out into the backyard?

Could she really have done all of that in her sleep?

5

KEERA CAME over that afternoon. "I called Stella and Lauren. Neither of them got music boxes or anything else from the Haunted Museum," she reported. "Show me this music box."

Emma and Keera went upstairs to Emma's room where the music box still sat on her nightstand. Keera picked up the music box, turning it in her hands to examine it. "It looks okay now," she said, opening the lid. "But you said the little figures were spinning around like crazy?"

"Yeah, and the music played way too loud and too fast."

"Maybe it's just broken."

"Maybe," Emma allowed. "Mom thinks I dreamed the whole thing, but my feet were dirty, which kind of proves I was outside."

"These little dolls aren't doing anything freaky now."

"What about the eyes I saw on the other side of the mirror?" Emma asked.

Keera smiled. "It was *you*, silly."

"No, it wasn't," Emma insisted. "The eyes were *blue*, and it was definitely someone else looking at me." But she was starting to wonder if it *had* been her own reflection she'd seen last night. Maybe her eyes had just looked different because the lights weren't on.

Keera shook her head and turned the key to begin the music. Emma had to admit that the lilting waltz was pretty. As they both listened to "The Blue Danube," Emma began to sway to the melody.

Soon she was gliding and turning across her bedroom floor as her mind filled with the music. There was no room for thinking about mysteries or creepy eyes or music boxes. She wasn't even thinking about her movement. Emma was simply at one with the notes of the piece.

Keera clapped when the music box wound down and the melody faded. "Emma, how can you say you're the worst dancer in your class?" she asked. "The way you just danced was awesome."

"Thanks," Emma replied. "The music box is really nice to dance to. But if I were with the others in my class, I'd be bumping into them and stepping on their feet."

"That's kind of hard to believe. You were so graceful."

"Believe it," Emma said firmly.

"Did you decide if you're going to audition for the dance team?" Keera asked.

"I don't see the point of bothering. I won't make it."

"You don't know unless you try," Keera argued. "And you love dancing. Wouldn't it be fun to do?"

Emma flopped onto her bed. "It would be great to be on the team. The girls go to dance competitions and performances. They win trophies and travel around the country. They even go to big cities and perform with professional dance companies."

"So do it," Keera urged. "You just needed to find the right piece of music, and 'The Blue Danube' is totally your song. Fate brought this music box to you," she said, growing excited by the idea.

"I don't believe in fate."

"Fate, good luck, you know what I mean," Keera insisted. "Promise me you'll at least try out?"

"Okay — promise," Emma said.

Keera and Emma went downstairs to watch some movies and forgot about the music box.

But later that night, after Keera left, Emma opened the box and saw immediately that the little male doll had fallen to the bottom of the box.

Emma lifted him up and gasped. His eye was unmistakably rimmed in black, as though someone had hit him! And the little woman doll now had her head thrown back and looked as if she was laughing wildly.

Emma stared at the music box so intently that she jumped when she caught a motion out of the corner of her eye.

Jason appeared at her door. "What are you doing?"

"Come here, Jason. Look at this."

"Cool," he said, examining the male doll. "How did you do that?"

"I didn't do it," Emma said. "The woman doll attacked her dancing partner."

"Oh, yeah? How dumb do you think I am? You twisted those figures just to scare me. How did you get them to bend? Did you melt them or something?"

"I didn't! I just found them like this."

"Very funny, Emma!" Jason left, chuckling gleefully. "The marker under the doll's eye was a good touch, though."

"Pest," Emma muttered.

Emma tossed the little man into the music box and slammed it shut. She ran from her room, calling to her parents. "Mom! Dad! Come here!"

Alarmed, her parents hurried upstairs. "Emma, what on earth has incited such an outburst?" Mr. Bryant asked.

Emma opened the music box. "Look at this! The little woman doll hit the man and now she's laughing about it. He's got a black eye! See for yourself."

Her parents peered into the box and then exchanged a worried look. Emma quickly checked. The little man and woman were standing beside each other once more, just as they'd been when she first opened the box.

Emma stared into the music box, stunned. How had *that* happened?

"They weren't like that a minute ago," she insisted. "Ask Jason."

"Jason!" Mr. Bryant called. "We require your presence and assistance for a moment."

Jason came up the stairs into the hallway. "What's going on?"

"Emma is of the opinion that her new music box is displaying some peculiarities," Mr. Bryant explained.

Jason cast a confused look at his mother.

"Something's strange about the music box," she explained.

"Oh." Jason looked into the music box. "Hilarious, Emma," he said drily, looking at her. "You twisted them and now you've untwisted them."

"I didn't do that, Jason!" Emma said. "You know they looked different."

Mrs. Bryant put her arm around Emma's shoulders. "You've had a long day and that Haunted Museum has spooked you," she suggested.

"I told you that I didn't approve of her admission to such a place," Mr. Bryant added as he and Jason headed back downstairs.

Maybe they were right. It was possible that the museum was making her imagination work overtime.

"Let's get you to bed," Mrs. Bryant said, continuing to guide Emma back toward her bedroom. "Everything will seem better in the morning."

Emma nodded, hoping her mother was right. As she headed toward her room, Emma heard her father and Jason speaking at the bottom of the stairs.

"Uh-oh," Jason said with a sigh. "I hope Emma's not cracking up — again."

6

THAT NIGHT, Emma slept fitfully. Had she really imagined everything the music box was doing?

This sort of thing had happened before, back in the third grade.

That year, her teacher had been the super strict Mrs. Clatter, a terrifying woman with no patience who didn't seem to like her job very much. She'd always seemed on edge and was constantly yelling at the class to sit down and be quiet even when they were already behaving just fine. Their work was never up to her standards, and homework assignments that had never been assigned were requested to be turned in. Mrs. Clatter had made Emma so nervous that she'd had nightmares about her teacher every night and dreaded going to school.

Then, because she was so tired all the time, Emma was clumsier than ever. The kids laughed every time she tripped or knocked something over.

Every morning, Emma's heart would race with anxiety. Each afternoon, she came home and cried. One day, Jason found himself accidentally locked outside of the house and was leaning on the doorbell to be let in. Already sleepy and anxious, Emma imagined that Mrs. Clatter was coming to take her away. She ran out of the house, hysterical with terror, and it took Emma's mother and some neighbors four hours to find her.

That was when Mr. and Mrs. Bryant really began to worry.

They took Emma to a therapist who prescribed tiny pills to calm her down. Emma *did* feel better after taking them for a while, though the nightmares didn't truly go away. But the only thing that really worked was when school ended for the summer and Emma was on her way to the fourth grade. Once Mrs. Clatter was out of her life, things got so much better that Emma didn't even need the little pills anymore.

But was it happening all over again?

Was Emma so nervous and upset about the dance team audition that her mind was once again playing tricks on her?

Emma got out of bed, slipping into a pair of flip-flops. Her parents might still be up. If they were, she wanted to talk to them about her worries. Maybe she should take the little calming-down pills again. She also wanted to see if she could convince her father to bring the music box to the school where he worked and toss it away. If it was that far from the house it might not be able to find its way back.

Emma was halfway down the stairs when she heard her parents talking in low tones. When she heard her name mentioned, she quietly backed up the stairs so she could listen without her parents becoming aware of her.

"It could be that Emma requires a calming respite at a facility equipped to handle such singular behavior," Mr. Bryant remarked.

"I don't know," Mrs. Bryant said warily. "There's one nearby, but it's for teens, isn't it? Do you think that would help Emma?"

"One of my students recently returned from some time at the residence, and seems much improved."

"I heard Mrs. Clatter has left teaching and is the new dean of girls over there."

Mrs. Clatter!

Emma could hardly breathe.

There was no way Emma was going to any place run by Mrs. Clatter!

"Don't you remember how much Emma disliked her?" Mrs. Bryant added.

"Oh, that was long ago." Mr. Bryant dismissed the concern. "I'm sure that Mrs. Clatter is in a much more pleasant professional situation. Besides, Emma probably does not remember her former instructor."

But Emma certainly did remember. Hurrying back to her room, Emma shut the door, trying not to panic. The music box sat closed on her nightstand, just as she'd left it. She couldn't let it get to her. There had to be a way to get rid of it without mentioning it to her parents. It would only convince them further that she needed to go away, to the place run by Mrs. Clatter.

Emma decided that she had to return it to the Haunted Museum on her own. She checked her phone and saw that if she got off the bus she took to dance class one stop early, the Haunted Museum wasn't far from there. She'd simply walk in and give it back.

Emma yawned, rubbing her eyes. She felt calmer now that she had a plan. She took a glass paperweight from her desk, placed it on top of the closed music box, and settled down to sleep.

• • •

In the middle of the night, Emma rolled over and her eyes fluttered open. Something was pulling her out of a deep sleep.

Da-da-da-da DUM Dee-dum dee-dum Da-da-da-da DUM Dee-dum dee-dum

"The Blue Danube" was playing.

"What?" Emma sat up, rubbing her eyes as she came fully awake.

The lid of the music box was open on her nightstand. The paperweight was back on the desk. Hadn't she put it on top of the box?

The little man and woman were spinning on their platform. They looked fine, as if nothing had happened to them.

Da-da-da-da DUM Dee-dum dee-dum Da-da-da-da DUM Dee-dum dee-dum

This is a dream, Emma decided. At least she hoped it was.

Lifting the box, Emma examined it in the light of the moon. Startled by what she saw, she threw the box onto her bed.

The eyes were back! Once more, the blue eyes peered through the oval mirror.

Emma crawled onto her bed, afraid to look at the mirror inside the lid, but determined to know if it was really her own reflection. Holding the box at arm's length, and at an angle so that she was definitely not reflected in the mirror, Emma got her answer.

These were *not* her eyes.

Someone was looking through the mirror.

"Hello?" Emma whispered. "Who are you?"

Once more the music swelled, and the little figures began to spin faster and faster. At the same time, a gray mist seeped through the oval mirror and poured into the room.

Emma slammed the lid shut, looking around her room frantically to see where the mist had gone. As suddenly as it came, it seemed to have disappeared.

Getting out of bed, she found two belts in her

closet. She buckled one and then the other around the music box. Nothing could get out of that. And right after school tomorrow she was taking this thing back to where it had come from.

A rustle came from the corner, and once more Emma searched the room for any sign of the creepy mist. "Is someone in here with me?" she asked in a quivering voice.

A low howl filled the room.

Emma dashed to her bedroom door, her hand on the doorknob.

Then she remembered Mrs. Clatter.

Her window was open a crack. Outside, she could see trees swaying. "It's just wind," she whispered to herself. Emma went to the open window and shut it. "Just wind."

She stood a moment in her silent room and listened. There was no more howl. No more "Blue

Danube." Convinced things were calm, Emma climbed back into her bed, pulling the covers up.

Emma lay in bed for a while, wide-eyed, listening. Slowly her heart slowed down and sleep overtook her.

After several hours, Emma awoke as a gentle breeze crossed her face.

Lifting onto her elbows, she looked around the room. Everything seemed quiet — but the window had been opened.

7

THE NEXT day, Emma moved over to let Keera take her usual spot beside her on the school bus. "What's in there?" Keera asked, nodding at the paper shopping bag between them.

"I'm taking the music box back to the Haunted Museum after school," Emma explained.

"How will you get there?" Keera asked.

"If I get off the bus one stop before I usually

would, I can walk to the museum, give this back
to them, and then head to the dance studio."

"Are you sure you want to give it back?" Keera
asked. "It's so pretty."

"Do you want it?"

"Uh . . . no."

"See?" Emma said. "You think it's weird, too."

"Maybe," Keera admitted. "Kind of. I
don't know."

The music box sat, belted closed, in Emma's
locker all that day. Every time she opened her
locker, she was relieved to see it wasn't up to any
new mischief.

After school, Emma took the bus downtown
toward her dance class.

The ride went as it always did, passing a horse
farm and then an old, abandoned barn as it traveled
closer to the mall that housed the dance studio.

Emma tried to get her pre-algebra homework done during the ride, though this day it was hard to keep her mind on it because she was nervous about returning the box.

What would she say to the Haunted Museum people about the music box? Maybe they wouldn't even take it back. If so, she'd simply leave it there.

Two stops before the bus reached the Haunted Museum, a boy she'd never seen before got on the bus. Emma decided instantly he had to be some kind of celebrity. His dark hair and eyes, coupled with his lean, athletic good looks, made him seem really extraordinary. To her utter amazement, he slipped into the seat beside her.

"Hi," he said with a smile. "By any chance, can you tell me how to get to Madame Andrews's dance studio?"

"That's exactly where *I'm* going," Emma

replied, trying not to sound as flustered as she felt. "How did you know?"

"You look like you could be a dancer," he explained. "And you're carrying a dance bag."

"We'll be there in four more stops," Emma said.

"Well, I guess I can just follow you now."

"Yeah, sure you can," she agreed. All thought of getting off the bus early flew from her head.

"I'm Roberto," he introduced himself, and she noticed he spoke with a slight accent.

"My name's Emma. I haven't seen you at the studio before. Where are you from?"

"Milan, Italy. My dad's Italian but my mother is American. Dad had to travel for work so I'm staying here with Mom for the rest of the school year."

He told her he was in eighth grade in a different school from Emma's and this was his first day of dance class. "I signed up for the hip-hop class but they said I had to have some background in ballet and modern dance to be allowed into hip-hop. They only had room in an intermediate class. I hope I can keep up."

"I'm in intermediate ballet/modern!" Emma said excitedly.

"That's great!" He seemed happy that they were going to be together in class.

At the third stop, the bus took on more passengers. The Haunted Museum was only two blocks away. Emma rose to get up but froze, unsure whether to stay with Roberto or head to the museum. Roberto was so cute!

But she didn't want to spend another night with the music box, either.

The bus driver made the decision for her by pulling away from the stop.

"Have you ever been to that Haunted Museum place?" Roberto asked, glancing at a billboard as the bus drove past it.

"Yes, just this weekend," Emma said. "It seemed pretty cheesy — but then they sent me a music box that I think was from the exhibit. It seems . . . broken. . . ." Emma wasn't sure how much to tell him about the music box, because she didn't want him to think she was silly or odd. But he seemed interested, nodding and asking questions.

"Strange," he said. "Can I see it?"

"Yeah, of course." Emma lifted the box from the bag and opened it, hoping that the little dancing figures would be doing something truly bizarre to prove her point. But they stood there, looking perfectly respectable.

"What was it you said this music box was doing?" Roberto asked.

Emma suddenly regretted telling him anything about the box. "It just gives me the creeps, that's all."

Roberto wound the box and smiled when "The

Blue Danube" began to play. "This is so beautiful," he commented, watching the little figures dance.

When he looked up from the music box and caught Emma's gaze, a dazed expression formed on his face. It was as though he was seeing Emma for the first time, and he was mesmerized by her. "It's not as beautiful as you are, though."

His remark startled her. "Me?"

"I could just look at you forever and never get tired of it," Roberto went on.

"I'm sure you would . . . get tired of it, that is," Emma said lightly. His compliments were sweet, but they seemed to come out of nowhere. It was as if he'd fallen under some sort of spell!

8

JUST AS Emma had expected, once they got to class and Madame Andrews introduced Roberto, all the girls clustered around him. Emma made sure to sit a little closer to him on the dance floor, as if to call dibs because she'd walked in with him.

As the class started warming up, though, Emma wished she'd stood on the other side of the room. She was humiliated whenever she bumped into someone or stepped on another dancer's toe.

She glanced at Roberto each time to see if he'd noticed her clumsiness, but he never appeared to be looking.

Roberto picked up the dance steps with an athletic grace and ease that impressed everyone, including her. She recalled how well she'd danced to the "The Blue Danube" back in her room when she'd played it for Keera. If only she could dance that well now!

Madame Andrews nodded along as the students practiced, and then clapped her hands. "Very good, class. Now, each of you will present the work you've been doing on the ballet leap known as the jeté. Line up in the corner of the studio and jeté on a diagonal across to the other side."

Emma could feel the blood drain from her face. If she could have found a way to escape, she would've been slipping out the studio door at that very moment. It was bad enough to bumble her way through class, but to dance alone in front of everyone was too much. The thought of tripping herself up — as she'd done several times — was just too embarrassing. If Roberto had thought she was *amazing* before, this would put an end to his admiration.

Emma slunk to the back of the line, hoping class might end before it was her turn. She wasn't at all surprised when the class star, Elizabeth McGowen, volunteered to go first and did a perfect jeté. Elizabeth's two best friends, Stephanie and Olivia, went next and they were nearly as good. A few girls took the safe route and did jetés that were only tiny hops forward, but they didn't stumble or fall. Even Roberto, who was new to ballet, succeeded.

Finally it was Emma's turn. This was going to be a total humiliation.

And then the pianist, Roger, stood up. "I have

to leave for my doctor's appointment, as we discussed, Madame," he announced. "Good night, Madame Andrews, class."

"But, Roger, Emma's the only one left," Madame Andrews objected. "Couldn't you stay a few more minutes?"

"That's fine by me," Emma said to Madame Andrews. "I don't mind. Really! I don't!"

"You'll have to do it without music," Madame Andrews told Emma. "I want to know that you've mastered the jeté before the dance team auditions."

I haven't mastered it. I could just tell you the truth. And that would save us both a lot of trouble, Emma thought.

"She has music," Roberto spoke up, heading for the pile of Emma's belongings in the back of the dance studio. He quickly found her music box, unbuckled its belts, and wound it.

"Wonderful," Madame Andrews said as the notes from "The Blue Danube" floated up from the music box. "Go ahead, Emma."

Emma edged forward. The buzz of chatter that usually filled the room while the girls waited for their turn to dance had stopped. All eyes were on her. Someone giggled.

For a moment, the urge to run was nearly overwhelming.

But then Emma's feet began to tingle. Just as it had back in her bedroom, the music lifted Emma, making her sure-footed and graceful. She leaped, and was confident that she was flying higher than she ever had before.

When Emma reached the center of the studio, she felt so charged with the thrill of the dance that she stopped and broke into a series of rapid pirouettes, spinning strongly, even without the cushioning of pointe shoes.

Emma saw the others reflected in the mirror, gawking at her in amazement. Even Madame Andrews wore a stunned expression.

Only Roberto didn't seem surprised by her performance. He once again gazed at her with that rapt adoration he had worn on the bus while "The Blue Danube" played.

Emma saw all this from the corner of her eye as she turned and turned. But then a new sight caught her attention. It was her reflection in the floor-to-ceiling dance mirror behind her.

The girl who was dancing so superbly there wasn't Emma!

Everyone was so busy watching Emma that they weren't looking at her reflection in the mirror.

As the music box sputtered to a stop, Emma faced the dance mirror. For the briefest moment she saw what was there.

The ballerina in the mirror wore a red ballet costume with a tutu covered in sequins. It glittered as she twirled. A golden tiara sparkled on her raven hair.

Why couldn't they see the reflection of the ballerina? Was Emma the only one who could?

And those eyes.

Those were the eyes that had peered in on her through the music box mirror!

Emma stumbled off the tops of her toes, staring at the image.

"Emma!" Roberto yelled with alarm as Emma toppled to the floor.

"Ow!" she cried in agony, clutching her ankle. It throbbed horribly. Was it broken?

Emma glanced back at the mirror, but the ballerina was gone. All she could see was a puff of misty gray smoke.

9

So? Did the Haunted Museum take back the music box?" Keera asked that night as Emma spoke to her on the phone. Her mother had insisted she stay in bed with her ankle wrapped in an Ace bandage and propped on a pillow.

"No. I had to call my mom to come pick me up. After I twisted my ankle, there was no way I could take the bus home on my own."

"Does it hurt a lot?"

"It hurts like crazy."

"Sorry."

"Thanks."

"Tell me more about this Roberto guy," Keera said.

Emma suspected she had changed the subject to get Emma's mind off the pain. "Like I said, he's really, really cute. And nice! Since he was waiting with me when Mom showed up, Mom drove him to his house. He asked for my phone number. He's already texted me tonight to find out how I'm feeling."

Keera squealed with excitement. "Awesome!"

"I know."

Emma considered telling Keera about the ballerina she'd seen in the dance studio mirror. But it sounded so bizarre! Keera would probably tell her that she was upset about not being able to get rid of the music box.

"Is the music box behaving?" Keera asked, as though sensing what was on Emma's mind.

"Keera, do you believe me that there's something strange about it?"

"I believe that *you're* convinced it's strange."

"But you think I'm imagining it?"

"Maybe," Keera said. "It makes more sense than mist coming out of a mirror and dolls that move by themselves."

Could that be true? Was Keera right?

Emma gazed at the box on her nightstand. It certainly wasn't doing anything weird now. She hadn't opened it since the class.

"Emma? Are you going to be in school tomorrow?" Keera asked.

"No. I have an appointment in the morning to see some kind of bone doctor to check out my ankle."

"All right. Text me when you get out of the appointment to tell me what he says. I'll check my phone during lunch."

"Okay," Emma agreed. Talking to Keera had made her feel better. All things considered, it hadn't been such a bad day. Even though her ankle throbbed, she didn't think it was broken. She'd met Roberto, who seemed to like her. And she had even impressed the other dance students with her performance. A few had congratulated her on it and had seemed friendlier than usual.

If only that strange ballerina hadn't appeared in the mirror. Emma still didn't know what to think about her. She thought of the mist in her bedroom the night before. It had been in the mirror, too. Was there some connection?

Mrs. Bryant stuck her head in to check on Emma. "The swelling has gone down," she noted, studying her daughter's ankle. "Does it still hurt?"

"A little. Mostly when I stand on it."

Mrs. Bryant nodded thoughtfully. "Get a good night's sleep and we'll find out how bad it is when we see the doctor. It would be a shame if you couldn't try out for the dance team next week."

"It would be," Emma agreed. It struck her now that she *wanted* to be on the dance team. Until this moment she hadn't admitted to anyone — even to herself — how much it mattered to her. And after today's performance, it suddenly seemed possible.

"I'm glad you've changed your mind," Mrs. Bryant said with a smile.

"I have, Mom. I really have."

Mrs. Bryant kissed Emma on the top of her head. "Good night, dear. I hope your ankle will be all better in the morning."

"I think it will be."

As Mrs. Bryant was leaving, Emma's phone buzzed with a new text message. It was from Roberto! *Hope you're feeling better. Sweet dreams. Talk to you tomorrow.*

She texted back. *Thanks. You too. Talk tomorrow!*

Turning off her lamp, Emma settled into bed and drifted to sleep with her lips curved in a smile.

• • •

Emma woke suddenly, three hours later, and froze in terror.

A ghostly woman was standing beside her bed!

Her red dance costume glinted in the moonlight and gray mist swirled around her legs.

Coming more fully awake, Emma realized it was the ballerina from the mirror.

The ballerina glowered down at Emma. "Get up! Now!" she commanded. "You can't steal my music box and hope to get away with it. Who do you think you are?"

Emma blinked. Who was this person and how had she gotten into her house?

"Mom! Da —!" Emma's voice was cut off as the ballerina clapped her hand over Emma's mouth. With her free hand, the ballerina tugged at Emma's wrist with a viselike grip.

"You are coming with me." Emma detected a Russian accent.

"No! I'm not," Emma insisted, attempting unsuccessfully to yank back her arm.

With one hand still over Emma's mouth, the ballerina grabbed at the music box with the other. The music box moved — by itself — away from her hand. Each time the ballerina tried to grab for it, the music box moved.

Emma stared at the box, wide-eyed with amazement. How was the music box moving? It seemed to have a life of its own. And it was determined not to let this ghostly ballerina get ahold of it.

With startling strength, the ballerina hauled Emma off the bed. "I see what's happening," she snarled. "You're its new master. It only wants to serve you now. Well, we'll see about that."

Emma rubbed her mouth, which ached from the pressure the ballerina had put on it. "Take the music box," she said. "It's yours. I don't want it."

"It doesn't matter what you want," the ballerina replied. "It's what the music box wants that counts."

"All I did was touch it."

The ballerina studied Emma, and her eyes narrowed. "I see. You're coming with me, then." She smeared a dark, gooey substance on Emma's arm.

"The Blue Danube" was playing faster now. Lit by the moon's rays, the little dancers were keeping pace, twirling madly as the music grew louder.

The ballerina reached into the box, touching the oval mirror with her finger, and a misty fog swirled around her. The grip on Emma's arm was released as the woman dissolved into the spinning vapor.

Emma sighed with relief, sure she was free. But before she had the chance to even move, she, too, dissolved into a vapor and was pulled, as if by a powerful tide, into the oval mirror.

Emma stood on a large stage in an old-fashioned theater. Her ankle didn't hurt anymore; it was as though the injury had never even happened.

The ghostly ballerina was beside her, clutching the music box with one hand. She'd lost her misty appearance and now seemed fully real. Onstage, ballet dancers, male and female, were dressed as if for a fairy-tale ball.

A man in tights and a flowing white shirt instructed a line of six pairs of dancers on how to do a waltz. The couples were dressed as if they were attending a royal ball. From the costumes and the music playing, Emma realized they were performing *The Sleeping Beauty* by the composer Tchaikovsky.

The director noticed the ballerina and Emma standing there. "Hurry, Alexa!" he called. "You're late! Change for Act Two!"

"I'll be right there," Alexa the ballerina responded as she began to drag Emma away from the stage.

"Hey, somebody help me!" Emma shouted toward the stage. "Stop her!"

But the man had gone back to his dancers and didn't appear to even hear Emma. None of the dancers paid any attention.

"Let me go!" Emma demanded, struggling.

"Be quiet," the ballerina barked.

Emma wondered if she could scream loud enough to be heard over the music that had started playing, but Alexa was already tugging her away and it was too late.

Alexa pulled her to a dressing room with the ballerina's name on the door and shoved Emma inside, onto the floor. "If you utter a sound, it will be the last one you ever make," Alexa threatened.

Emma sprang up and ran for the door, but Alexa slammed it shut, throwing her body in front of it. "I need you near me until I can figure out a way to get the music box to serve me once again. What do you mean you touched it? It was here with me."

"I was in the Haunted Museum."

"The what?" Alexa snapped.

"It's a museum with strange stuff in it. I don't know how it could be in two places at once. It's haunted, I guess."

Alexa stared at the music box. "Maybe it wasn't in two places at once. I haven't been able to find it for the last two days. Then I saw you through my ballet dance mirror and discovered where it had gone to."

"I didn't ask for it to come to me. It just appeared," Emma told Alexa.

"It does have strange powers." As Alexa spoke, the music box disappeared and reappeared in Emma's hand — as if it had jumped invisibly between them. "How did you do that?" Alexa cried.

"I didn't do anything!" Emma answered. "The music box is acting on its own."

"Don't try to get away. Until I can make the music box mine once more, I'm keeping you close.

There's no sense fighting. The music box used to serve *me*. And I have to find a way to make it serve me again."

Alexa shoved Emma down into a chair and the music box jumped into her lap, its lid opening on its own. Forcing herself to peer inside, Emma saw that the little dancing couple stood calmly on their springs.

Alexa turned a knob on a gas lamp that raised the flame inside its glass globe. Emma watched, fascinated, even though she was terrified. Why were they using such an old-fashioned way of lighting the room? Where *was* she?

Alexa gathered up a blue dance costume that was draped on a velvet couch and disappeared behind a changing screen.

Turning slowly, Emma studied the room. Besides a table, the couch, and the changing screen, there was a mirrored vanity with a purple-cushioned bench in the far corner. It was strewn with an assortment of makeup pots, brushes, combs, and some tools Emma had never seen before. The walls were covered in theater posters for various ballets in a number of cities. One poster in particular caught Emma's eye.

ALEXA OPENSKAYA IN HER EXCITING DEBUT DANCES THE ROLE OF THE SLEEPING BEAUTY. DON'T MISS THE BALLET EXPERIENCE OF A LIFETIME.

The performance was dated August 4, 1892.

Eighteen ninety-two! They'd gone back in time more than one hundred years!?

Emma saw another poster on the floor, though it was torn and crumpled. It was identical to the one on the wall except that it listed a different ballerina in the lead role. SONIA RU — Emma couldn't make out the name that had been ripped away.

What had happened to this ballerina named Sonia?

Alexa emerged from behind the screen in her costume. The blue tulle skirt, the jeweled top with its puffed sleeves, and the glittering diamond tiara made her look a perfect Sleeping Beauty at the ball. Her satin toe shoes glittered. Emma couldn't believe how such an evil being could appear so beautiful.

"Why does my music box suddenly favor you?" Alexa demanded. "How did you get it to come to you?"

"I've told you! I didn't take it — it just arrived. I don't even want it."

Alexa's face reddened with fury. "Don't lie! You summoned it!"

"Maybe the Haunted Museum stole it, but I didn't."

"The Haunted Museum!" Alexa gasped. "Why do you keeping talking about that?"

"Everyone knows the —"

"Miss Openskaya, they're waiting," a male voice called from the other side of the door.

"I'll be back to deal with you in a little while," Alexa said in a threatening snarl. She glared at Emma as she opened the door and swept out. Emma heard a key lock the door.

A sudden thud sounded from inside a closet. What could have caused it? What else could be in the room that Alexa shared with a creepy music box?

The door of the closet swung open slowly.

"Hello!? Who's there?" Emma called.

Sнннн!" a female voice hissed.

Emma looked up at the person standing in front of her.

A young woman had emerged from the closet. Her blond hair was swept into a simple bun, and she wore a long, high-collared dress with lace around the neck. "Please be quiet. I don't mean any harm, and we don't want Alexa to come back!"

"Who are you?" Emma asked.

"Lucy Smith."

The girl's voice was friendly, and Emma breathed a little easier. "Where are we?" she asked.

"We're in Boston, of course," Lucy replied. "Why aren't you wearing proper clothing?"

Emma was self-consciously aware that she was wearing a huge old T-shirt that had been her dad's. Her hair was disheveled, and she had no shoes on. "I was asleep when Alexa brought me here."

"Is that all you sleep in?" Lucy asked. "A man's shirt?"

Emma nodded, recalling old pictures she'd seen of women sleeping in long, white, ruffled nightgowns.

"You poor girl," Lucy said. "I'm sure you have enough problems without Alexa in your life."

"Not a fan?" Emma asked.

"A what?"

"You don't like her much," Emma clarified.

"I should say not!" Lucy replied.

"Why were you hiding in her closet?" Emma asked.

Lucy blushed and stepped closer to Emma, lowering her voice to a conspiratorial whisper. "I'm not supposed to be in this room."

"Then why were you?"

"I was searching for —"

The color drained from Lucy's cheeks when she noticed the music box, which had slipped onto the floor. One hand flew over her mouth as she pointed at the music box with the other.

"The music box?" Emma asked.

Nodding, wide-eyed, Lucy wilted onto the couch as though the sight of the box had made her feel faint with fear.

Without either Emma or Lucy touching the music box, it slowly opened.

"How is it even doing that?" Emma asked in a small, frightened voice.

Lucy shook her head in bewilderment as "The Blue Danube" began its lilting melody. "I haven't the slightest idea," Lucy replied, her voice quaking.

Emma clenched her fingers, fearful of what she'd see next. "Have you seen what this thing can do yet?" she asked.

"I have," Lucy said. "I'm fairly certain it killed Sonia Rubenya."

Suddenly energized, Lucy sprang from the chair and threw herself onto the music box, desperately trying to shut the lid. "Stop it! Don't let it play!"

Emma knelt at Lucy's side, helping her to press down on the lid as it opened ever wider. They threw all their strength into it but they weren't able to push it closed.

"We have to get away from it," Lucy said urgently as she got to her feet. "When it acts like this, anything could happen."

12

Lucy produced a ring of keys from the pocket of her long dress and unlocked the door. Suddenly the music box launched itself into Emma's arms. "I guess I'm stuck with it for now," she said. "But let's get away from Alexa while we can."

The backstage area was a maze of hallways, but Lucy knew her way. As they ran, Emma looked down and realized she was no longer holding the music box. Where had it gone?

They heard the sound of "The Blue Danube" and followed it through the corridors until they emerged into the theater's wings. *Da-da-da-da DUM Dee-dum dee-dum Da-da-da-da DUM Dee-dum dee-dum*

The music drew Emma's eyes to the stage. The music box was now on the floor.

The ballet dancers, so beautifully costumed for the ball in *The Sleeping Beauty*, were all onstage, spinning and leaping at top speed. Some moved so fast they were a mere blur. The music was impossibly loud, and played faster and faster as she listened.

Emma glimpsed the director with the flowing white shirt and ballet tights jumping high into the air — over and over again — as though he were on a spring.

Alexa stood in the middle of the stage, turning in rapid pirouettes and paying no attention to the mayhem around her. Her face radiated blissful happiness, and Emma could hardly look away from her flawless dancing. But she was moving too fast.

Emma watched, stunned, as Lucy lifted the music box, which sat playing at an ear-shattering volume in the middle of the stage.

"I think the music box is helping us escape," Lucy said as she watched in amazement. "It's working to help you. You're its master."

"Come on! Let's get out of here!" Emma shouted.

The stunned expression left Lucy's face, and she dropped the box as she ran with Emma down the stage's side steps and through the center aisle.

Emma and Lucy finally slowed their pace when they were five blocks from the theater. They were leaving the entertainment district of Boston and heading toward a more residential section where stately, multistory houses with quarter-acre yards stood in respectable rows.

Emma panted hard. "What do you know about that music box?" she asked Lucy, bending forward to catch her breath.

"Just what I've seen. My house isn't far from here. Let's go there and I'll tell you everything."

Soon they came to a large, three-story wooden house with a fence around it. "Tell me more about the music box," Emma requested.

"My parents wouldn't like it if they knew I was working at the theater," Lucy said, heading toward a bench in her yard.

"Why not?" Emma asked as they sat side by side.

"Theater people," Lucy replied. "They're not really respectable."

"Even ballet dancers?" Emma asked, surprised.

"They're slightly better regarded than actors, I suppose. Still, it's not a place to be. If my parents find out, they'll be furious. They're very strict. I'd like to be a ballet dancer myself someday, though my parents would never allow lessons. That's why I was so happy when Sonia Rubenya agreed to let me be her assistant."

"I love the ballet, too," Emma said. "For some reason, the music box made me a better dancer. Maybe it would help you to dance, too."

"Do you think so?" Lucy questioned.

"I don't know," Emma replied. "You can have it if you want it. I don't want it."

"Thank you," Lucy said. "But it seems to have a mind of its own. Besides, we left it back at the theater. Who knows if we'll ever see it again?"

Emma wasn't sure how to feel about that. It was a huge relief to be rid of the music box. But now she was stuck back in time, away from her family and friends. Did she need the music box to get home?

"Tell me everything you know about the music box," Emma said.

"One day, the music box just appeared in Sonia's dressing room. It was in a wooden box and the return address was in London, from some place called the Haunted Museum."

Emma gasped. "The Haunted Museum!?"

"You know it?" Lucy asked, surprised.

"There's one by where I live."

"There's more than one?"

"Yes! It's a chain. I think so, anyway."

"A what? What kind of chain?"

"A bunch of Haunted Museums. They're all over the country."

"Really?" Lucy shook her head. "Well, Sonia had just come back from London. Perhaps that was where she encountered the music box. But no one in the theater had ever heard of a Haunted Museum. I asked everyone. We advised her to send it back, but Sonia loved the music box. Before, Sonia had been in the corps de ballet. Once she had the music box, she became a principal dancer — a star! — almost overnight."

"Did her music box play 'The Blue Danube'?" Emma asked.

"Yes! It was exactly like the one Alexa had. Sonia insisted that they use 'The Blue Danube' in the scene of *The Sleeping Beauty* at the ball, even though it isn't in the original score. She insisted that the music director use the waltz for the scene."

"Did she dance better all the time, or only to 'The Blue Danube'?"

"It was the strangest thing," Lucy replied. "It was just as you said before — it made her a superb dancer. Sonia was a wonderful dancer to begin with, but when she danced to 'The Blue Danube,' she really soared. People were starting to say she had become the greatest ballerina in the world! And Sonia insisted that the music box always be hidden onstage somewhere, playing. She refused to dance without it there."

"She wanted the music box there even though she had a whole orchestra to play it?" Emma questioned.

Lucy nodded. "The orchestra drowned out the music box, of course. But still, Sonia demanded that it be playing. It was my job to make sure it never wound down while she was dancing."

"And did you ever see it do anything weird?" Emma asked.

Lucy trembled, and a paleness came to her face as she nodded. "You wouldn't believe some of the things it did. I thought I was going insane at first."

Just like me, Emma recalled. "I know how you felt."

"I wonder if *anyone* could know how I felt. It was so terrifying. Sonia didn't care, though. The only thing that mattered to her was the fame the music box brought her."

"Something obviously went wrong since she's not in the ballet now. What happened to Sonia?"

"One morning, Sonia didn't come out of her dressing room," Lucy continued. "When they finally went in to check on her, she was slumped over her vanity table. When we tried to wake her, we made a terrible discovery. She was dead!"

"What had happened to her?" Emma asked, horrified.

"The official explanation was that she danced so much that it wore her out. She danced until she dropped. It killed her. She danced herself to death."

"What happened to the music box?" Emma asked.

"The police said she must have used her last dying breath to hide it. That doesn't make sense to me, though. I suspect that Alexa must have come into Sonia's dressing room and taken it. And now, since she had it before you, I'm certain. Suddenly *she* became a great dancer."

"Well, now the music box is gone."

"I wish we hadn't left it behind. Maybe I could have been a prima ballerina if we still had the music box and you were willing to give it to me."

"If you really wanted that music box, and it was up to me, you could have it," Emma said. "But it's gone now, so never mind."

"It would have made me a great dancer and my dream would have come true," Lucy said unhappily.

Emma realized Lucy was right. "I get it now," she said. "The music box makes its owner a great dancer. When I danced to its music it was as though it took hold of my feet and made them dance in a way I never could do on my own. There was an enchantment in that music box."

"An evil enchantment," Lucy added. "You saw what it was doing to the dancers at the theater."

"Maybe, but it would have made you a great dancer, just the same."

Lucy stood. "I'll bring you out something warmer to wear. Stay here. I'll be right back." She seemed sad, as though she regretted leaving the music box behind now that she thought about how it might have made her ballet dreams come true.

Emma watched Lucy go into the house, her shoulders slumped with disappointment. Emma was feeling equally low. She didn't want to stay in 1892. She'd miss her family and friends —

especially Keera. And Roberto! She'd barely gotten to know him.

The bench she was on suddenly buzzed with a vibration. Surprised, Emma looked around and gasped.

The music box was back, sitting on the bench, without a scratch on it.

13

EMMA SAT on the quilted bedspread that covered the creaky old-fashioned brass bed in Lucy's room. Lace curtains fluttered gently in the breeze from the slightly open window.

Both of them stared at the music box, which now sat in the middle of the bed. At the moment it seemed peaceful enough — just an ordinary music box.

"I can't believe it came back," Lucy said as she paced.

"It seems to have a way of doing that," Emma remarked, thinking of how it had mysteriously returned from the garbage can. "I could have sworn the garbage truck carted it off, but it showed up back in my room."

"I don't understand," Lucy said. "Garbage what?"

"Lucy, you might not believe this, but, I'm not . . . from here."

"What are you talking about?" Lucy asked, completely puzzled.

"I know it sounds unbelievable, but it's true. Somehow, Alexa dragged me through this little mirror." Peering into the oval mirror, Emma saw only her own eyes peering back at her.

"Is that possible?"

"I know it doesn't sound possible," Emma admitted. "But she appeared in my room and then turned herself into a sort of vapor."

"Perhaps we should go back to the theater," Lucy said.

"And talk to Alexa!?" Emma yelped. Why would they ever want to see *her* again?

"She might know how going through the mirror works. After all, she was able to do it to get to you."

"That's true. But she's so scary."

"If we stay together, we can handle her," Lucy said.

"She's so strong, though," Emma said. She wondered if Alexa's amazing strength came to her from the music box. Now that they had it, would they be stronger than Alexa?

"You would really give me this music box?" Lucy asked.

"If it was in my power to give it to you, I definitely would. Really," Emma said.

"Let's get another look at it." Lucy picked it up from the bed and lifted the lid.

"Do you think that's a good idea?" Emma asked doubtfully.

"How else will we figure out how to get you home?" Lucy said as she wound the key to start the music.

"Good point. I don't know."

The music of "The Blue Danube" filled the room. Lucy set the open box with its gently spinning figures back on the bed.

Da-da-da-da DUM Dee-dum dee-dum Da-da-da-da DUM Dee-dum dee-dum

The sound of that music panicked Emma. "Close it, Lucy! Close it right now."

"No! You gave it to me. It's mine now!"

"We don't know whose it is yet," Emma argued. "It might still be mine, and I'm saying to keep it shut."

Emma was so caught up trying to persuade Lucy to shut the music box that she didn't even notice when the pace of the music first began to speed up. But the strange vibration caught her attention and she jumped away from the bed, startled. The vibration's buzz grew louder and louder. "What's happening?!" Emma cried, her voice trembling.

Lucy had flattened herself against the wall by the door. "I — I d-don't know!"

The music was becoming unbearably loud, and the girls clapped their hands over their ears, cowering away from the noise. Then, tiny male dolls began to stream from the box; their frantic shouts were a high-pitched whine.

"They're getting bigger!" Emma cried, terrified, as the small music box men began to grow.

Lucy lunged for the door and rattled the knob. "It won't open!"

The little woman doll stepped out of the box last. She'd already grown to full size, and was bent forward, laughing.

"The Blue Danube" blasted.

The room was filled with the music box men, who shuffled around, seeming not to know where to go.

Emma found Lucy and gripped her arm.

"What do they want?" Lucy cried frantically.

"I don't know!" Emma said. "Let's get out of here."

The music box men and woman knocked books from the shelves and threw furniture across the floor. They didn't seem to want anything but to destroy everything in their path, and they slowly made their way toward the girls, who were cornered against the door.

"How can we get out of here?" Lucy squealed. "The door is stuck fast!"

The music played even louder, and it seemed to make its way into Emma's brain. It made the room spin. Emma clamped her hands over her ears again as colors spun inside her head. She had to make it STOP!

HAD TO MAKE IT . . .

had to . . . make it . . .

had to . . .

stop

14

WHEN EMMA opened her eyes, she was on the floor in the bedroom. Her forehead ached, and when she touched it, she flinched from the pain. Something had hit her, or maybe she'd simply fallen down and banged her head.

Where were the music box creatures? Where was Lucy?

The only thing Emma could think to do was to head for the theater. She hoped she remembered the way. The thought of going back there terrified her. But what other choice did she have? The scary ballerina, Alexa, was the only one who knew about the music box, and Emma couldn't think of anyone else who might know what the music box men had done with Lucy — or how to get her back.

Emma tried the door and was happy to find it was no longer locked. She made her way through the silent house. All the furniture was broken and thrown around. The paintings on the walls were now on the floor. It was clear that the music box people had made their way through, destroying everything they touched. She hoped Lucy was all right.

In less than fifteen minutes, Emma was within several blocks of the theater and could see the building. On the outside, everything looked quiet enough.

The front door was locked, so Emma went around to the side. Stretching high on tiptoe, Emma looked through a first-floor window into a hallway. A shadow slid across the wall. Someone was in there!

The window was halfway open. Emma wondered if she could squeeze through.

It took a small jump for Emma to get to the window ledge and pull herself up. It was tight, but Emma managed to maneuver through until she was in.

Emma stood in the hallway, breathing hard and wondering what to do next. Frightened though she was, there was no going back now. She hurried through the hallways until she came to the main stage area. From the wings of the theater, she stared.

All the other people from the stage were gone. Only Alexa stood onstage, dressed in her blue tulle

Sleeping Beauty costume. Emma stepped out onto the stage to confront her.

"You!" Alexa cried angrily. "Where have you been? Have you brought me my music box?"

"It's not yours," Emma said. "It belonged to Sonia Rubenya."

"But Sonia couldn't handle it," Alexa replied. "She let it possess her until it danced her to death."

"It would have done the same to you," Emma told her.

"No, it wouldn't," Alexa disagreed. "I'm stronger than Sonia was. I could have controlled the music box."

"How would you do that?" Emma asked.

"By giving my heart and soul to it," Alexa replied. "All I want is to be the greatest dancer alive. The music box can do that for me. And the music box protects me. As long as I am its master it will stop anyone who attempts to get in the way of my greatness."

"But I possess the music box now," Emma stated firmly.

"No one possesses the music box," Alexa countered. "*It* possesses the dancer of its choice. All it cares about is the dance. It chooses the one who is the greatest dancer."

"That's why the music box chose me," Emma pointed out to her.

"You? A dancer? Ha!" Alexa scoffed. "Greater than I am?"

"Maybe not now, but someday I might be," Emma said.

Alexa folded her arms defensively. "The music box does what it needs to do on *my* behalf."

"Then why did it come to me?" Emma asked.

Alexa scowled at Emma. "You touched the

box. You broke the bond. The music box no longer wanted me. It found you."

Fury swept across Alexa's face. "Do you know what it's like to trip on your own feet when only hours ago you were the greatest ballerina in the world!? I had to get that box back. I tore through Sonia Rubenya's diaries looking for all I could uncover about the music box. Then, one day, I discovered the way."

"What did you find?" Emma asked.

"Sonia wrote about the day she first saw the music box in a little building called the Haunted Museum while she was in London. She picked up the music box to examine it and was sharply scolded by the owner of the place, a woman wearing robes and heavy jewelry. Her name was Belladonna Bloodstone."

Emma gasped. She remembered seeing that name over the front door of the Haunted Museum:

OWNER BELLADONNA BLOODSTONE. She must have been a descendant of the original owner.

"When Sonia returned to Boston, the music box was delivered to her," Alexa continued. "She assumed that the strange Miss Bloodstone felt bad about scolding her and was making a gift to apologize."

It wasn't difficult for Emma to make the connection between this story and her own.

"After Sonia died, I just knew that the music box was responsible for her sudden greatness," Alexa continued. "I was the first one to find her dead in her dressing room. I took the music box and hid it so no one else would find it. In no time, I became a prima ballerina. I was dancing like a dream, and then suddenly it disappeared, and I could barely take two steps without stumbling."

Emma realized that the day she touched the music box in the Haunted Museum must have been when it left Alexa and came to her. "How did you find out it was with me?" Emma asked.

"I traveled all the way to London to find Belladonna Bloodstone in her Haunted Museum. I told her that the music box had abandoned me but that I could see, in my dance mirror, where it was."

"Where was it?" Emma asked.

Alexa colored red. "It was with you, of course. Idiot!"

"When you told her this, did she think you were insane?" Emma asked.

"Not at all," Alexa replied, calming down. "She wasn't one bit surprised. Miss Bloodstone sold me a potion that allowed me to come through the mirror to get you and the music box."

"But we went *through* the music box," Emma said, puzzled.

"It doesn't matter. Wherever the music box's master is, that's where it goes," Alexa explained.

Da-da-da-da DUM Dee-dum dee-dum Da-da-da-da DUM Dee-dum dee-dum

Emma looked sharply toward the back of the theater where the familiar music was playing. "And here I am," Lucy said as she walked down the center aisle, holding the open music box. "The little dancers consider me their master now."

"Impossible!" Alexa cried. "You!?"

Lucy nodded. "Look at this!" Still holding the open, playing music box, Lucy twirled gracefully down the aisle as she spun in rapid turns, and then leaped high through the air. "I could never dance before," she said with a mix of delight and disbelief. "Not even a little. I just *wanted* to be a dancer."

Lucy clutched the music box to her chest. "Give us the potion you bought from Miss Bloodstone. I was standing in the back. I heard what you said. Let Emma go home through the mirror."

"Never!" Alexa shouted.

Lucy slowly opened the lid of the music box. *Da-da-da-da DUM Dee-dum dee-dum Da-da-da-da DUM Dee-dum dee-dum*

"You are standing in the way of what I want," Lucy threatened.

ALL RIGHT! All right!" Alexa gave in, backing away. "Follow me."

Lucy and Emma trailed Alexa to her dressing room, where she took a jar of black waxy goop from her vanity table. "*That's* the potion?" Emma said to Lucy in a whisper.

"It had better be," Lucy replied.

"Come with me," Alexa commanded. They

followed her to a dance rehearsal room in the theater. A floor-to-ceiling mirror covered the far wall.

Alexa faced Lucy. "If I send her back, do you promise to give me the music box?"

"Do you promise not to hurt people with it?" Lucy replied.

"I can't control the music box," Alexa said. "It has a mind of its own."

"If you can't control it, you shouldn't have it," Emma said.

"Lucy, if I don't have your promise that you will give me the music box, you will never get this potion," Alexa insisted, holding the jar of black goo over her head.

"Really?" Lucy asked calmly as she grabbed for the jar in Alexa's hands and got it away from her. "How do I use this?"

"I won't tell you!" Alexa snapped.

Da-da-da-da DUM Dee-dum dee-dum Da-da-da-da DUM Dee-dum dee-dum

"You're annoying me again," Lucy said, holding the lid of the music box ajar to let it play.

Alexa scowled and jumped in an attempt to get the jar back, but Lucy was taller and she couldn't reach it. Emma grabbed Alexa's arms. Without the strength from the music box, Alexa couldn't break free.

"You rub the potion on your wrists," Alexa answered reluctantly.

Lucy handed the jar to Emma, who opened it and immediately turned her head away. "What a stink!" she exclaimed.

She smeared the goo on her wrists and waited. Emma's whole body tingled, and she felt somehow less solid.

Suddenly dizzy, she staggered toward the mirror.

The room spun.

Emma's right arm melted into a stream of white vapor. "Oh!" she shouted. It was so scary to have her arm disappear like that.

Da-da-da-da DUM Dee-dum dee-dum Da-da-da-da DUM Dee-dum dee-dum

It was the last thing Emma heard as she melted completely into vapor.

· · ·

Emma strained to see in the jet-blackness that engulfed her. Where was she?

From the hallway, a light clicked on. Instantly Emma saw that she was in Madame Andrews's dance studio.

Relief flooded her. She was home! But she wasn't alone. Had the music box people come through with her?

"Who's out there?" Emma called.

Roberto came into the studio. "Emma!" he cried, thrilled to see her. "Are you all right?"

Emma examined herself in the mirror. All her body parts had made it through. She patted herself thoroughly, just to be sure she was solid. "Yes! I'm fine!"

"Everybody is out looking for you! A group met up here to organize a search party. I only came back to get my backpack." He held up a key ring. "Madame Andrews lent me these so I could let myself in. She's out searching, too. What happened to you?"

"How long have I been gone?" Emma asked.

"You've been missing for most of the day. Don't you know that? Where were you? Why didn't you call or text anyone?" He lifted his cell phone to display the many texts he'd sent trying to find her. "Did you lose your phone or something?"

"You'll never guess where I've been," Emma said.

"Try me."

"I was in Boston, in 1892," Emma said, still not quite believing it herself. "They didn't have wireless back then, so I couldn't answer my phone. How could you ever guess that?"

"No, that's not something I would have guessed," Roberto agreed, staring at her with a puzzled expression. "Did you fall, maybe? Something has affected your brain."

Emma didn't know what to say. How could she expect anyone to believe what had really happened? It might be easier to tell everyone she'd fallen and then wandered back to the dance studio.

"How did you get into the dance studio?" Roberto asked as they headed for the front door. "The place was locked when I got here."

"Uh . . . I don't know," Emma said. "It's all so foggy. I just don't know."

"Why are you dressed like that?" Roberto asked, taking in the long gown Emma still wore.

It was time to think fast. "Uh . . . the last thing I remember is the school play. I was trying out for it and they asked me to wear this costume. That's the last thing I remember."

"Maybe you tripped on the long hem," Roberto said.

"Yeah, that's probably it."

When they stepped through the door, Roberto took out his phone and called Emma's parents. "They'll be right here," he told her.

"Do you think you're well enough to try out for dance team tomorrow?" Roberto asked Emma as they waited for her parents to arrive.

"No. Definitely not."

"But you're so talented." Emma realized that

Roberto wasn't looking at her with that crazy gaga expression he'd worn when the music box was playing.

"Maybe you could dance to your music box again," Roberto said. "You danced so well to it the other day."

Emma imagined how it would be if she had the music box back. "I'm not really sure what happened to that music box," she told him.

"Really? That's too bad. Do you want me to help you look for it?"

"No. Don't worry. I never really liked that thing anyway."

Of course, she was happy that the music box was gone.

But was she? Really?

"WHERE HAVE you been?" Emma's mother cried when Emma climbed into the backseat of the family car. "Are you all right?"

"I'm fine," Emma said. "Hungry." She realized she hadn't eaten all day.

"We were so worried! You didn't answer your phone, and that nice boy, Roberto, came by and said you hadn't showed up in dance class. What are you wearing?"

Emma glanced in the rearview mirror of the car and caught sight of the ruffle-collared old-fashioned gown of Lucy's she wore. "I was in Boston! In 1892. I thought I'd never get home. That music box had a real ballerina in it, who appeared in my bedroom last night. She pulled me back through time and —"

Her father sat behind the steering wheel and scowled at Emma's reflection in the mirror. "Don't be fresh, young lady. Where were you?"

"I just told you!" Emma said.

Mr. Bryant's expression became even sterner. "Emma," he said in a warning tone.

"You must have gotten up very early because I didn't see you this morning," Mrs. Bryant said, trying to smooth things over. "Is that your costume for dance class?"

"Yes. We were trying to see if I could dance in this," Emma lied. "I tripped on the long hem and fell. I hit my head and have been wandering around all day in a kind of fog."

"Oh, dear." Mrs. Bryant fretted. "I hope you don't have a concussion. We're taking you right to the hospital. You need to be looked at."

"Really, I just want to eat and go to sleep. Please," Emma pleaded.

"We'll get you something to eat after we go to the hospital," Mrs. Bryant replied.

Emma'd tried to be truthful with Roberto and he didn't believe her — and now her parents doubted her story, too. Emma knew she'd have a hard time believing the truth herself. Luckily she was wearing the long gown Lucy gave her. It proved — at least to herself — that she hadn't dreamed the whole thing.

At the hospital, a doctor had Emma stand on one foot as he pulled on her hands. They put her under a machine called a CAT scan, and then finally released her, stating that she was fine.

When they got home, Emma felt exhausted. She wanted to go straight to bed, but she noticed a pad lying on the table. Her mother had written down the words *Five Arrows Youth Facility*, and a phone number.

There was no way she was going anywhere that was run by Mrs. Clatter!

Emma devoured the cold chicken she found in the fridge and then headed for her bedroom. It had been one exhausting day. Leaving the long, dirty gown in a heap on the floor, Emma flopped onto her bed, the music of "The Blue Danube" playing through her mind. Would she ever be able to forget it?

In the middle of the night, she woke with a start.

Da-da-da-da DUM Dee-dum dee-dum Da-da-da-da DUM Dee-dum dee-dum

Frantically she peered into the darkness.

Da-da-da-da DUM Dee-dum dee-dum Da-da-da-da DUM Dee-dum dee-dum

The moment she snapped on her lamp, the music drifted away. Had it been a dream? Or was the sinister box back?

Emma got out of bed and looked around her room. The music box wasn't anywhere to be seen — nor was it under her bed, in her closet, or in a dresser drawer. She'd dreamed it.

That was a relief. Wasn't it?

Emma tucked herself back under the covers and turned the light off once more. Shutting her eyes, she quickly fell into a dream in which she turned and turned on a stage, dressed as an elegant prima ballerina, dancing *en pointe* while the audience in the immense theater stood and applauded and shouted *Brava*. A graceful leap landed her in Roberto's arms, and he held her high over his head.

• • •

"Have you told anyone else about what happened?" Keera asked Emma the next morning as they rode the bus to school.

Emma shook her head. "Who would believe me?"

"I do." Keera looked at Emma, stared out the window, and then looked back again. "Well, sort of."

"You think I'm lying?" Her best friend didn't even believe her — that proved she shouldn't talk about it.

"Not lying exactly, but . . ."

"But what?" Emma asked.

"There was that time back in third grade, when we had Mrs. Clatter . . ."

"That was Mrs. Clatter's fault, not mine!" Emma said. "She drove me crazy."

"Yeah, but she actually drove *you* crazy. No one else in the class needed therapy, even though we all hated her. And you *have* been acting strangely lately. Where were you really yesterday? Did you cut school?"

"I told you what really happened."

"It's easier to believe that you cut school than you went back in time and were chased around by tiny people who came out of a haunted music box," Keera said.

"I know," Emma admitted. "But it *is* what happened and I'm *not* losing my mind."

Keera sighed and looked worried. "Well, I think you're right not to be talking about it in school. Did you tell your parents?"

"I tried to. My dad just thought I was being bratty. Mom already has the phone number for Five Arrows on speed dial. Mrs. Clatter is now running it."

"Uh-oh!" Keera said, wincing. "You don't want to land there."

"That's for sure."

"Definitely don't tell anyone what happened. Just forget about the whole thing."

"I will," Emma agreed. She closed her eyes to clear her mind.

Da-da-da-da DUM Dee-dum dee-dum Da-da-da-da DUM Dee-dum dee-dum

If only she could get the music out of her head.

THE LIST of those who have made the dance team is posted on the wall by the piano," Madame Andrews announced that afternoon in dance class. Emma sat with the other students on the dance studio floor. Roberto was nearby, but talked quietly with the three other guys in the class. Everyone looked over in surprise to the paper tacked to the wall.

"But we didn't even audition!" one of the students cried.

Madame Andrews smiled. "The class before last was your audition," she replied. "I thought I'd spare you the stress of a formal tryout."

The class filled with grumblings of complaint.

"If I'd known, I would have done better."

"You didn't give us a chance to practice."

"I didn't have my good dance shoes with me that day."

Madame Andrews quieted everyone with a wave of her hand. "If you're not always putting forth your best effort, then you have no business being on the dance team. Wouldn't you agree? And if you didn't make it this time, there's always next year to try again.

"Take a few minutes to check the list and then we'll start class," Madame Andrews told them.

The ballet students scrambled onto their feet to see the results of the tryouts. Instantly the wall by the piano was swarmed with the dancers, some crying out happily, others sighing with disappointment.

Emma stayed seated, her stomach clenched. What if she hadn't made it? It would be so embarrassing if Madame Andrews thought she wasn't a good-enough dancer to be on the team — all she wanted to do was dance!

"Aren't you coming?" Roberto was standing next to her, his hand outstretched.

Emma took it and he drew her up. "I'm sure *you* made it," she told him. "I'm not as confident about me."

"I bet you did — your dancing was great. Let's go see."

The crowd around the list had thinned out,

and Emma found Roberto's name in moments. "Congratulations," she said. "You're in!"

"Thanks, but all four of us guys made it," Roberto replied. "There aren't enough male dancers for Madame Andrews to turn any down." He leaned in closer to the list and pointed. "There you are. You made it, too. Awesome!"

She'd made the team! Until that second she hadn't been willing to admit aloud how very, *very* much she'd wanted this. Emma beamed, and Roberto twirled her around.

The other students who'd also made the team smiled and even hugged her. For the first time ever, Emma felt as if she belonged in the class. And it was a great feeling.

Madame Andrews clapped her hands to resume class. "Setting aside the dance team for now, this year for our recital we'll be performing various scenes from the ballet *Swan Lake*.

Today I'd like all the girls to work on some chore-ography for the lead part of Odette, the swan princess. You boys will learn the part of Prince Siegfried."

Emma glanced quickly at Roberto. He was — by far — the most prince-like of all the boy students, and in a few weeks he would no doubt be the best dancer, too. He was sure to get the Siegfried part.

That meant she *had* to be Princess Odette! She didn't even want to *think* of him dancing such a romantic role with another girl. Emma had to be the best of the girl dancers. She decided that she'd practice as much as she had to in order to get the part. For a moment she was caught up in the dream she'd had — dancing with Roberto, the wild applause, the glitter of sequins and ballet shoes as she glided effortlessly and flawlessly through the pas de deux. . . .

"What's wrong?" Roberto asked her. "You look like something's bothering you."

"I was just thinking it would be cool if you and I could be Odette and Siegfried," she confessed. Her face felt warm and she hoped she wasn't blushing.

Roberto nodded. "That would be fun. I'm not sure about me, but you have a great chance of getting the part."

"No, I don't."

"Are you kidding? You're the best one in class."

Emma remembered how well she'd danced to "The Blue Danube." With the music box, it was as though her feet were dancing on their own, possessed by the music. Roberto had never seen the old, fumbling Emma, who'd tripped herself up before the music box had come into her life. And maybe he never would.

Madame Andrews separated the boys from the girls and taught each group the opening steps they would have to know to dance the leads. When she left the group of girls to go instruct the boys, each dancer was left to practice the steps on her own.

Emma did her best to reproduce the steps Madame Andrews had shown them. "Hey, watch out, Emma!" Elizabeth grumbled as Emma accidentally slapped her.

"Sorry!" Emma apologized, shocked by her own clumsiness.

"Ow!" shouted Stephanie when Emma stumbled into her.

"Stop fooling around over there," Madame Andrews scolded.

"Tell Emma," Olivia complained. "She's the one causing the trouble."

This time Emma knew she was blushing. It was so humiliating — and in front of Roberto! Without the music box, she was more out of step than she had been before she had it.

She'd thought she hated the music box, but now Emma longed for its power. "I'd give anything to have that music box again," she said softly.

AFTER CLASS, Madame Andrews asked Emma to stay behind for a moment. "I'll wait for you outside," Roberto offered.

"Okay. Thanks." She was happy he was still willing to be seen with her after the way she'd embarrassed herself.

Madame Andrews waited for everyone to leave before speaking. "Emma, I want you to know that

I was seriously considering you for the role of Odette."

"Really?" Emma gasped happily.

"Yes, but listen to me. I based that decision on the improvement you've shown recently. If your performance is as sloppy as it was today, I won't be able to put you in the role. You can't be crashing around here as if you're in your own world. You have to work with the other girls."

"I can! I will!" Emma assured her.

"I want to see the graceful, balanced dancer I know you can be. No more of the lazy dancing I saw today. Promise?"

"Oh, I promise. I'll work really hard."

Madame Andrews smiled at Emma. "Good. I'll see you next class. Practice!"

"I will. Thank you!" she said as Madame Andrews walked out of the dance studio.

"Yes!" Emma pumped her fist in the air.

She was going to dance the lead role in *Swan Lake*. And most likely it would be with Roberto. Awesome!

Unless . . .

Unless she wasn't good enough, and Madame Andrews picked someone else for the role.

Why hadn't she brought the music box back through the mirror with her when she had the chance?

As Emma thought this, a gray vapor began to waft up from the bottom of the floor-to-ceiling mirror.

Emma stepped toward it. What was going on? Should she get Madame Andrews?

Roberto tapped on the door frame. "Ready to go?"

"Look at this," Emma said, pointing to the fog. "This is how it started — when I was pulled through the mirror!"

Roberto stepped into the room, staring into the mirror. "I don't see anything, Emma. And I don't want to, either. Everything that you said happened sounded so strange. I'd rather forget about it."

Emma peered through the fog. Was something there? Yes. A blurry figure was definitely moving behind the mist. Was it dancing? Yes. It was. Why couldn't he see it?

"Maybe you're right. You go ahead," Emma told Roberto. "I'm going to stay and practice some more."

"All by yourself?"

Emma stepped toward the mirror almost without meaning to, feeling almost hypnotized by the dancing figure. Something about it was drawing her in. "Madame Andrews is still in her office," she told Roberto, her voice growing dreamy as the mist worked its spell on her. "I won't be alone."

"Okay," Roberto agreed reluctantly. "Are you sure you're all right?"

"Mmm-hmm," Emma assured him.

"Bye, then."

"Bye, Roberto."

Emma was so mesmerized by the misty figure that she barely noticed Roberto leave. As she moved closer to the mirror, she realized that the figure wasn't in the steam. It was in the mirror!

A quick check over her shoulder confirmed that there was no one else in the studio. This wasn't a reflection.

When Emma was so close that her nose nearly touched the glass, she could clearly see the scene in front of her. It was as though she was standing at the back of a stage, watching the dancers in a ballet from behind.

The prima ballerina was lovely as she danced across the stage. From her blue-and-white costume,

Emma recognized that she was playing the role of Cinderella.

Was it Alexa?

No. Emma decided that the ballerina was too tall to be Alexa. This was some other dancer.

The stage was different, too. It was far larger and more elegant than the one they'd been on.

Why was she seeing all this? What did it mean?

The curtain fell and the applause in front of it was thunderous. Cinderella and the prince stepped forward to bow. The crowd's cheers grew deafening. Bouquets of flowers flew through the air.

The two stars of the ballet backed away from the stage as the crowd continued to cheer. Slowly the ballerina turned so that Emma could see her face.

It was Lucy!

Emma stumbled back, stunned. How had Lucy become such a great dancer in so short a time?

The music box!

The music box was making her a great dancer. "That's my music box," Emma whispered into the empty studio. "It came to *me*."

Emma watched as Lucy took three curtain calls. An emotion arose in her that she'd never experienced before. It made her belly hurt. She couldn't think straight.

"It's my music box," she spoke again. "That should be me on that stage."

Emma could see Lucy racing through the back hallways of the theater until she reached her dressing room. Once inside, she locked the door and leaned on it, panting, her hand over her heart. "Unbelievable!" she said breathlessly. "The music box has done it again."

The music box sat on Lucy's dressing table. She wound it, and then opened the lid. *Da-da-da-da DUM Dee-dum dee-dum Da-da-da-da DUM Dee-dum dee-dum*

Lucy gazed down into the box. "Stop that!" she cried. "Stop it!"

Emma realized that the tiny dancers in the music box must be fighting, just as they had when she'd owned the music box. The thought of them made her smile now. How silly the tiny creatures were. She'd been foolish to be afraid.

Suddenly Lucy screamed.

Emma stepped forward, eager to see why.

A pair of eyes was staring at Lucy through the oval mirror on the inside of the music box lid. It was exactly the same as the time when Emma had seen Alexa staring at her.

"Huh!" Emma gasped. All at once, Emma knew whose eyes they were.

Lucy was seeing Emma staring back at her in the music box mirror.

19

THAT EVENING Emma knelt on her bedroom floor using a kitchen knife frantically to scrape the black goo from the cuffs of the gown Lucy had loaned her. The goo was getting dry, but a little water might turn it back into a paste. She would make it work. There had to be a way to get back through that mirror and get the music box. But how could she go through the mirror and bring the box back with her at the same time?

How had Alexa done it?

She'd forced Emma through and somehow the music box had followed. That was it! She'd force Lucy to come through with her.

Emma began working on the other sleeve. Soon there was about a tablespoon of the stuff smeared onto a plate at her side.

Someone knocked on her door.

Emma slid the plate and the gown under her bed. "What is it?"

Mrs. Bryant stepped into the room. "What's that smell?"

Emma remembered how much the goop stunk, though she'd grown used to it. "Oh, uh . . . my socks, I guess. I just took them off and threw them in the closet."

"Well, put them in the hamper. That's what it's there for."

"Okay."

Mrs. Bryant seemed to study Emma. "Are you all right?"

"Sure. Why?"

"You seemed agitated at supper and you barely touched your food."

"I had homework I needed to do."

"Then why aren't you doing it?" Mrs. Bryant asked as she looked around the room. She eyed her daughter's backpack, which hadn't moved from where it had been dropped on the floor a few hours ago. "I don't see any books."

"It's done."

Mrs. Bryant nodded, but she still seemed convinced that something wasn't right. "Why don't you come down and watch TV with the rest of us, then?"

Emma stretched and yawned. "I'd rather go to sleep early. I told you about how I might get the lead as Odette, remember?"

"Yes, that's very exciting."

"I know! So I want to really get a good night's sleep and stay rested so I can work hard."

"All right," Mrs. Bryant agreed. "Sleep well," she added as she left.

The moment her mother shut the door, Emma snatched the gown and the plate from beneath her bed. Her eyes widened with delight when she saw that some of the goop had also gotten on the gown's ruffled collar. "Excellent," she murmured as she scraped it off and onto the plate. "This should be enough."

"What are you doing?" Jason came through the door without even knocking. "What's that?" he asked, pointing to the plate.

"A science experiment," Emma lied. "Now, get lost."

Ignoring her, Jason settled on the end of her bed. "That doesn't look like any science experiment I've ever seen."

"It's black mold. I've been growing it in my closet. It's really deadly toxic, so you'd better get out of here."

"Oh, yeah?" Jason challenged, instantly off the bed and edging his way to the door. "What does it do to you?"

"It makes your skin rot and fall off."

"I don't believe you," Jason said. "You wouldn't be so close to it if that was true."

"I took the protective serum in school."

Jason continued looking skeptical, but he dashed out the door. Emma sighed in relief. Maybe she'd finally have some privacy.

Emma sat staring down at the plate of black ointment. Did she have to go back to the dance studio in order to get through to the other side or would any mirror do?

There wasn't much goop on the plate. She'd better not risk trying another mirror. She'd have to wait until tomorrow and hope the misty vision appeared a second time.

· · ·

The next day in dance class was just as awful as the day before had been. Emma stumbled through Odette's dance steps, and knocked herself and Olivia to the floor when she spun the wrong way. It didn't help that Madame Andrews seemed to be watching her all the while. And even worse — that Roberto kept glancing her way, wearing a worried expression.

"Do you feel all right?" he asked during their break.

"I'm sort of off today," Emma replied. "I didn't sleep very well last night." That was true. She'd been so nervous about what she was about to do next that she couldn't fall asleep.

"It's as if your mind is somewhere else," Roberto said. "Are you thinking about the music box?"

How much should she tell him? Emma wasn't sure.

"It's almost as if you've been hypnotized or are under a spell or something. I think you should try to forget about it," Roberto said. "Think of it as a bad dream."

"Sure. You're right," Emma agreed. "That's what I'll do." If only she could. But getting the role of Odette was too important to her — and she knew the music box was the only thing that could make that dream come true.

• • •

"I just want to put in some extra practice time," Emma told Madame Andrews after class that day. They had worked with the costumes at the

end of the lesson, and Emma felt like a true ballerina wearing a knee-length skirt made from
layer upon layer of multicolored tulle.

"All right. I'll be in my office if you need anything," Madame Andrews agreed as she left the
dance studio.

Emma quickly dug in her dance bag for the
black ointment, which she'd put in a plastic bag.
Then she stood by the mirror hoping desperately
that something would happen.

It didn't take long.

Once again, mist rose up from the floor, curl-
ing up the surface of the mirror. Emma stared as
the mirror turned gray and foggy, and then cleared
to show Lucy sleeping in an old-fashioned bedroom, likely in a hotel. The blue Cinderella costume
hung on a stand, off to the side, and the pointe
shoes twinkled in the pale glow from the window.

The music box stood on a night table beside

the bed. And it was open. Was it really possible that Emma would be able to come through the little oval mirror as a mist?

It seemed impossible, but Alexa had done it. Emma had to take the chance.

Emma scooped a small amount of black goop from the plastic bag and rubbed it on her wrists. The rest she tucked into the waistband of her dance skirt.

For a moment, she hesitated. Why was she doing this? It was too dangerous. It was crazy. Maybe *she* was crazy. But she needed the music box.

Her body tingled and her mouth went dry as she leaned into the mirror. Her mind quieted as it focused on one thing only. She had to become the greatest dancer the world had ever seen. Nothing else mattered.

Gazing at her outstretched hands, she smiled as they evaporated into a misty haze.

Da-da-da-da DUM Dee-dum dee-dum
Da-da-da-da DUM Dee-dum dee-dum

Emma heard the familiar notes even as she hung as a vapor in the air. Her form thickened and she could see herself once again. The soft glow of an oil lamp flickered, enabling Emma to make out Lucy's sleeping form in the four-poster bed.

In the music box, the little man and woman dolls were on their springs. Was she imagining it, or did they smile at her when she lifted the box to peer in? Emma was sure they did. They had missed her. After all, she was the true owner of the music box. They were simply putting up with Lucy while Emma was away.

Closing her eyes, Emma let the melody of "The Blue Danube" wash over her before twirling around Lucy's bedroom in a blissful trance. There was no stumbling this time. Her every step was in time with the music, each gesture elegant and lovely. Yes! It had been worth the risk of coming through the mirror to experience this perfection once more.

When the music box wound down and Emma stopped moving, Lucy was sitting up in bed, staring in surprise. "Emma?"

"Yes, it's me," Emma replied.

"Are you a ghost?" Lucy asked.

"A ghost? No! Of course not. Why would you ask that?"

"You look rather . . . . ghostlike."

Emma stretched her hands out and realized she could almost see through them. She recalled how Alexa had appeared when she first showed up in Emma's bedroom. Emma had also thought she was a ghost.

"I'm not a ghost, but I've come to take back the music box," Emma said, hoping her voice was firm. This wasn't a request. She was taking the music box no matter what happened.

Lucy clutched the music box. "No! You can't have it. It's mine!"

"It was mine first," Emma insisted.

"It belonged to Sonia Rubenya first," Lucy argued. "And it most likely belonged to someone else before that."

"Well, it's mine now," Emma said, her voice climbing with anger.

"I think not!" Lucy got out of bed. Holding the music box close, she faced Emma defiantly.

"I think so!" Emma grabbed for the music box and the two girls struggled, yanking it back and forth. Lucy finally pulled free, but Emma tackled her around the waist. Lucy fell hard onto the floor and the music box slid out of her grasp.

Emma pounced on it, covering it with her body. The power of the music box surged through her. She felt suddenly much stronger, as though she were absorbing the magic strength of the music box. It was truly hers now.

"Emma, don't do this to me. I thought we were friends," Lucy said, her face filled with distress. "I have a performance in the morning. It will be a disaster if I go onstage and can't dance."

Emma felt a wave of compassion for Lucy but it washed away quickly. "That's not my problem.

You couldn't even dance before you got your hands on the box. You're a fake. I've studied ballet since I was small. I deserve it."

"I can't believe you're the same girl I met before. What's happened to you?" Lucy asked.

Emma didn't want to listen anymore. Lucy was just trying to trick her. She got to her feet, still holding tight to the music box. "This is mine and I'm taking it back through the mirror."

"You won't be able to," Lucy said. "The music box will stay with me. I'm the one it wants."

"In that case, you're coming with me," Emma said, her voice nearly a growl. She'd never heard herself sound like this. It was frightening. What was happening to her? Emma shook her head to clear it. She didn't care what had happened. The only thing that mattered was that she would dance like an angel, and nothing could stop her success with the music box there to protect her.

Emma took the plastic bag of ointment from the waistband of her skirt and scooped out a bit of the goo. With a quick movement, she smeared some on Lucy's arm. "You're coming through, too — just to be sure."

"No!" Lucy shouted. "I have to dance tomorrow. I don't want to go with you. You've become a monster!"

Emma ignored Lucy as she put the goop onto her own wrist again. Gray mist swirled around the bedroom as both girls dissolved into fog.

Da-da-da-da DUM Dee-dum dee-dum Da-da-da-da DUM Dee-dum dee-dum

The music played louder and louder. The mist twirled itself into a ribbon of vapor and entered the oval mirror in the music box.

Emma was the first to come back to solid form on the other side. She still had the music box.

Lucy came out of the fog next. But Emma had no more need for her. Lucy was half solid, half mist when Emma used all her strength to push her by the shoulders.

Lucy disappeared back into the mirror.

In the dance studio mirror, Emma watched as Lucy tumbled into her hotel room. The moment she landed on the floor, the scene was gone.

Emma stared at her own reflection, breathless. The music box was beside her. Hers.

She'd won it!

"Are you ready to leave, Emma?" Madame Andrews asked from the doorway. "I'm locking up."

"I'm ready," Emma agreed, loading the music box into her dance bag.

"I'm glad to see you're working so hard," Madame Andrews said as they walked to the front of the dance studio. "You were kind of unsteady today in class."

"That's all over now," Emma said. "You're going to be amazed at my dancing from now on. I promise!"

E MMA, PLEASE sit still," Mrs. Bryant requested that night at supper. "Be seated and eat your dinner."

Still dressed in her leotard and dance skirt, Emma balanced into an arabesque, her back leg extended, before turning three perfect pirouettes around the dining room table. The music box sat on a stuffed chair in the corner of the room, playing. *Da-da-da-da DUM Dee-dum dee-dum Da-da-da-da DUM Dee-dum dee-dum*

"And silence that confounded music box," Mr. Bryant added. As though defying Mr. Bryant's order, it played louder, seeming to turn up the volume by itself. A light rain began to patter outside and on the roof, a perfect rhythm that accompanied the beautiful music.

"I'm so excited about *Swan Lake* that I can't sit still," Emma said, still dancing. "I'm sure I'll get the lead if I keep practicing, which is fine because I *love* to dance. I just want to dance and dance and dance. There's nothing else I'd rather do."

"Since when?" Jason challenged.

"Oh, since always. You know that. Dance, dance, dance. I've always been that way, I just never allowed myself to dance as much as I wanted to, but I've finally gotten serious about my career."

"What *career?*" her brother asked.

Emma noticed her parents exchanging worried glances across the table, but she ignored it. How could she expect them to understand the kind of passion that drove an artist to strive for excellence? After all, they were only ordinary people. They didn't understand the soaring glory of the ballet. They weren't gifted like she was.

"I asked you to cease playing that musical contraption," Mr. Bryant said more firmly, his voice getting louder.

In response, the music box increased its volume until it blasted so loud that Jason covered his ears, cringing. *DA-DA-DA-DA DUM DEE-DUM DEE-DUM DA-DA-DA-DA DUM DEE-DUM DEE-DUM*

Mrs. Bryant stood up. "Emma! Turn that thing off right now!"

Why would they want her to shut off the music

box? To Emma it could never be loud enough. Such a sweet sound. So beautiful. It was as though the melody was traveling through her like a warm, flowing musical river, and it made her dancing more dramatic and graceful. "Oh no! I never want it to stop playing. Not ever, never, ever. I want it to play all the time, so I can dance all the time."

Emma's father got up from the table and went to the music box. He slammed the lid shut, stopping the music.

Jason took his hands off his ears, sighing with relief.

Emma froze. Her parents stared at her as though she'd lost her mind. But they were the ones who didn't know what they were doing. "Why do you want to stop me from dancing?" she asked.

"Young lady, we are attempting to partake of a meal together," her father replied. "This is not an appropriate time for practicing one's hobbies."

"It's always time to dance," Emma said, growing upset. She needed her music so she could practice. She had to be Odette!

A buzz filled the room. The music box's lid had opened, and it was vibrating. "The Blue Danube" began to play softly, and Emma realized the music box was protecting her. It wouldn't let anyone stop her from dancing. Not even her own family. She swayed to the tune, letting it wash over her once more.

"Come on, Emma, cut it out," Jason said.

Emma looked down. Inside the music box there was now a crowd of little music box men — and they were starting to climb out. Just as they had back in 1892.

Soon they would fill the house, protecting her. Making sure nothing and no one stood between Emma and her dream — to be the greatest ballerina in the world.

One by one, the music box men came out of the music box. Her family hadn't even noticed them yet.

The music box was so loud now.

DA-DA-DA-DA DUM DEE-DUM DEE-DUM DA-DA-DA-DA DUM DEE-DUM DEE-DUM

The windows in the room cracked. A glass on the table burst into shards.

Emma's parents cringed, closing their eyes and covering their ears. Jason was under the table, his head tucked into his arms.

It didn't bother Emma, though. The music was wonderful. It couldn't be loud enough.

And then suddenly — she couldn't hear it at all. She spun and leaped in a world all her own. It was as though her feet had taken on a life of their own — moving faster and faster. Emma loved it. Was this what it was like to be a truly great dancer — to not even think of the movement but to become one with the music?

Emma no longer heard the music. She was in an ecstatic trance where nothing existed but the dance. Everything around her was completely silent. She was lifted by the rapture of her own movement.

But through it all, Emma could still see what was going on around her.

The music box woman now stood in the doorway, laughing, a terrible expression in her gleaming eyes. One by one, the music box men were growing larger and shuffling around the dining room.

The music box men began to surround her family. Mrs. Bryant fainted. Then Mr. Bryant passed out, his head down on the table. Jason still quivered under the table.

• • •

Emma blinked hard, as if waking from a deep sleep.

Her family was in trouble.

She couldn't let these creatures hurt them. Not even the chance to be the world's greatest ballerina meant more than her family.

The reality that her family was in danger hit Emma like a bucket of ice water, completely rousing her from the spell the music box had cast over her.

But the nightmare didn't go away upon awakening. It was still right there in front of her. The music box men continued to advance on her family. The music box woman still roared with sinister laughter.

What did these creatures plan to do to her family? How could Emma protect them?

22

FEELING AS though she was walking in a dream, Emma picked up the music box and held it over her head. The music box men and the woman stopped and stared at her.

Emma did a pirouette ending in an arabesque, and they moved closer — toward her, the master of the music box, and away from her family at the table.

In a series of grand jetés, she moved through the house. With the music box still held high, she danced out the door.

As she'd hoped, the music box men and the woman began to follow her. It was their job to protect her, wasn't it? That meant they had to be with her at all times. As long as she danced, they didn't have to protect her from anything.

But how long could she keep dancing?

Lightning flashed, though Emma couldn't hear any thunder. She still couldn't hear anything at all. A torrent of rain poured down on her as she moved through the streets, spinning and leaping.

The music box people followed, trudging along through the rain. Around them, people stared at the strange parade. Emma just hoped no one would try to stop them. Who knew how they would act if they felt threatened?

Emma's mind raced. She'd wanted to dance so badly, but now she was exhausted. Now she'd give anything to be able to stop. How was she going to get rid of this music box? No matter what she did, it would always come back to find her. Why had she ever gone back to get it? She'd been such a fool!

Emma spied a bicycle sitting in an open garage. Not knowing what else to do, she ran for it. She'd never stolen anything before, but she was desperate. The music box creatures growled and grumbled the moment she hopped on the bike, but they didn't stop following her.

Stowing the music box in the basket, Emma pedaled madly toward the Haunted Museum. It was her only hope.

In her deafened state, she didn't hear the horns honking at her or the wheels squealing as she led the bizarre group through the streets. Finally she reached the dark and locked Haunted Museum.

Emma found a side door and pounded to be let in. Maybe they could control the music box. At least they might know what to do.

As she pounded at the door, the music box began to vibrate, sending shock waves up Emma's arms. On its own, the lid opened. She knew "The Blue Danube" had to be playing, but she couldn't hear a single note. She felt a crawling sensation on the back of her neck, and knew what she'd see before she even turned around. The creatures surrounded her.

It was the last thing Emma saw before she fainted.

. . .

"Your parents will be coming to get you in a little while," Mrs. Clatter said to Emma. They were sitting in the main office of the Five Arrows facility, which really was a lovely place. Birds chirped outside the open windows, the sun shone down on a small pond on the grounds, surrounded by pine-needle paths and tall trees. Emma felt more peaceful than she could ever remember. "Is there anything else you'd like to talk about before you leave?"

Emma had been at Five Arrows for a week, and it really hadn't been so bad. She'd had a terrible cold from being passed out in the rain for hours before her parents had found her outside the Haunted Museum, slumped against the side door. They'd taken her to Five Arrows right away.

After two days, her hearing had returned. After that, she'd talked to counselors about why it meant so much to her to be the best dancer. They thought she'd imagined everything that had happened with the music box, even though Emma knew it had been real. No matter what she said, they kept insisting it had been some kind of delusion.

"Emma, do you understand what the counselors have been telling you?" Mrs. Clatter asked. "You seem to have returned to yourself, and we're happy you feel well enough to return home, but is there anything else you'd like to say or ask me?"

Emma took a deep breath to summon up her nerve. "Mrs. Clatter, why were you so mean to us when we were in the third grade?" she dared to ask. She just had to know. "I hated coming to your class so much it made me sick. I had nightmares that you were coming to get me. It was so bad that a doctor gave me pills to help me calm down. And I don't understand it." She felt that she could talk to Mrs. Clatter now. In the time she'd been at Five Arrows, she saw that the woman who had once been her worst nightmare had really changed.

"I'm sorry, Emma," Mrs. Clatter said. "Very sorry. That was an extremely difficult time for me. You see, I was never cut out to be a teacher. I'd wanted to change things for so long — and I took something from the Haunted Museum that I thought could help. It . . . didn't."

Emma stood. "Then you do believe me!"

"I do," Mrs. Clatter whispered.

Emma hugged Mrs. Clatter. It was great to know that someone believed her. Mrs. Clatter knew what objects from the Haunted Museum could do, too.

"Good luck, Emma," Mrs. Clatter said when Mr. and Mrs. Bryant arrived to pick her up. "Keep dancing, but only so long as you're enjoying it."

"I will," Emma said. "I'm in the troupe in *Swan Lake* at my dance school. It's not the lead, but I know it'll be fun." Madame Andrews had sent her an e-mail saying she was holding the spot open for Emma whenever she was ready to return to class.

"Let me know when the performance is. I'd like to come see it," Mrs. Clatter said.

As Emma walked out of Five Arrows with her parents, her cell phone buzzed and she saw that it was Keera. "Hi!"

"You won't believe where I am," Keera said over the phone. "Lauren is having her birthday party at the Haunted Museum. I'm calling you from the Haunted Music Boxes exhibit."

Emma went to speak but found that her mouth was too dry. She didn't want to ever think about that music box again.

"Remember that music box you were so scared of? It's sitting right where it was. I'm sure it's the same one," Keera went on.

There was no way Emma could have heard the tune under Keera's voice — but there it was, so faint that she wondered if she was imagining it.

Da-da-da-da DUM Dee-dum dee-dum Da-da-da-da DUM Dee-dum dee-dum

Licking her lips, Emma found her voice. "Listen to me, Keera," she said. "Whatever you do — DON'T TOUCH IT!"

ABOUT THE AUTHOR

SUZANNE WEYN lives in the heart of horse country, in a valley in New York State. She's the author of The Haunted Museum series, as well as the books *Reincarnation* and *Distant Waves* for older readers, and the Breyer Stablemates books *Diamond* and *Snowflake* for younger readers.

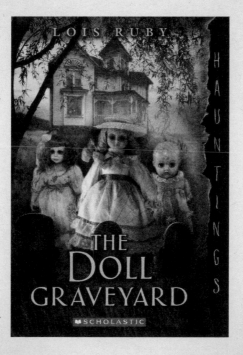

A SIX-BURNER STOVE!" Mom's still wigging out on kitchen appliances. "A side-by-side freezer/ fridge, and enough granite-slab counter space to do surgery."

Wow, you could get your appendix out while you wait for a baked potato. Personally, I don't care about kitchens. I'm moving right into the upstairs bathroom, since my own room is all red flocked wallpaper and a spindly, narrow bed with sagging springs that squeal every time you move an inch. Was this Emily Smythe's bedroom?

It must have been Emily's family who had the good sense to update the prehistoric bathrooms and kitchen in this creepy old house. Gram would have said they're to die for. Every muscle in my whole body is achy from pushing furniture around and hauling boxes up the stairs, not to mention hefting that kidney pie, so I lock myself and Chester in the bathroom and fill up the huge triangular tub with hot water and about a quart of bubble bath. It nearly overflows when I sink into the water up to my shoulders and just let my hands and feet float like they're weightless ghosts riding the bubbles and gentle waves. I can just feel stings of anger seeping out of me into the warm water.

Chester's chomping to jump into the tub with me, but then it *would* overflow, and chocolate-brown dog hair would clog the fancy new plumbing, so I tell him, "Hang on, pup. I'll take you out for a run later, okay?"

He whips his tail around, then coils onto the bath mat and snoozes patiently.

Not Brian. He's banging on the bathroom door. "I gotta go. It's an emergency!"

What a colossal pest. "There's a bathroom downstairs, Brian. It's the little room with the weird wallpaper that looks like old Sunday funnies. Oh, and it has a toilet. You can't miss it."

Finally I hear his footsteps stomping down the creaky stairs, but in two minutes he's back pounding on the door.

"Come on, Shelby. Mom says to take boxes up to the attic."

"Go ahead," I say lazily.

"Hunh-uh, not alone!"

"Okaaaay. Give me ten minutes, and we'll do the attic thing." Chester raises one ear in agreement that we'll just keep the pest waiting a lot longer.

· · ·

I've never lived in a house with an attic, and this one is the kind you have to move a rickety ladder up to, then slide the ceiling trapdoor aside and hoist yourself up onto the attic floor. Now I wish I hadn't. It's dark and smells like soured milk up here. I try to scramble to my feet till my head hits the ceiling. You'd have to be about the size of a shrunken Pygmy to stand up. That pink insulation fluff stuff sticks out between the wall slats. There's a small round window like the porthole on a ship, which gives a circle of light to the big, dark space that spans the whole length of the second floor of the house. Somehow that little bit of sunshine makes everything seem spookier, lighting up dust motes that swirl, though there's not a breath of a breeze. I think the air up here's stood still for about a hundred years.

Brian hands a bunch of flattened cartons up to me, and I slide them across the bare plank floor. The attic seems to be totally empty, but then one of the cartons sails across the floor and thuds into something with a peaked roof jutting up in the shadow. A dollhouse.

"Come up here, Brian." He scuttles up behind me, and we crawl over and push the little house across the floor toward the porthole, for a better look.

I ask, "Does this look familiar to you?"

"Kind of."

"Look here. Two windows with pale green lace curtains on each side of the front door. Four steps up, then a flat landing, then six more steps to the blue door. It's just like our house, even down to the goat-shaped knocker on the blue door."

"Same furniture inside, too. Cool."

Now I see the three green velvet couches circling the beveled glass-top table in the front parlor. Somebody built this dollhouse as an exact copy of the big house. Probably Mr. Thornewood built it for Sadie, the Tasmanian she-devil Mariah told me about.

The little house looks so lonely and abandoned. I wonder why Emily, or any of the other tenants, didn't take it with them when they moved.

Brian asks, "Where are the people?"

Good question. There's a mess on the floor, and the sink's full of those teeny dishes and pots and pans. It looks like everybody took off in a hurry. My eyes roam around the two stories of the house. "At least they didn't forget to take the baby, see? The crib's empty."

Brian chuckles. "Old-time toilet with the thing you pull instead of flush!"

"Not like our bathrooms, thank goodness. This dollhouse was probably built way back in the last century, and no one bothered to remodel it."

"Bathtub has claws, see?" Brian reaches in and pulls out the old-fashioned oval tub, then shoves it back in the dollhouse with a gasp.

"What? WHAT?" I yell.

He points to the bathtub. A tiny doll is floating facedown in a small puddle of water. Brian whispers, "They didn't take the baby."

"Let's get out of here." We both slide across the floor and scamper down the ladder super quick, then glide down the smooth banister to the ground floor, landing on a Persian rug that covers the hardwood. Chester's waiting for us. "Outside, both of you," I command. "It was stifling up there; we need fresh air." Brian tears out the front door, Chester right behind him, and I walk slowly, wondering if Sadie loved her dollhouse. I'm also wondering what kind of a kid would drown a baby in the bathtub. Crazy Emily?

Outside, I look up at dark thunder clouds rolling in. "We won't have much time out here before the rain starts. So enjoy it while it lasts."

The yard seems to be acres wide, but not much deeper than the house, and most of it is overgrown with weeds and tall grass. The only thing that saves it from being flat, ugly land are the twin mountains, the Spanish Peaks, dotting the horizon off in the distance. I'll bet they look really pretty dusted with snow. Something to look forward to, since we seem to be trapped here forever.

We pass a small fishing hole on the north side where no fish could survive in the mustard-yellow algae, and I think about fishing with Dad at Horsetooth Reservoir. *Don't go there,* I remind myself. *You're here, now* . . . where lots of weeping willow branches sag from the trees and brush the ground. The air is usually hot and still in late August, but those storm clouds are rolling in. There's a grassy clearing between two trees where someone seems to have chopped off the low-hanging branches. It looks strange in the middle of all that growth of weeds and grass and weeping willows. Chester sniffs the ground and whimpers. Maybe there's a juicy bone buried under there that he hasn't got the heart to go for right now, which is shocking, because Chester's a great digger. So

Brian and I move in closer to see what's stopped him. Chills ripple up and down my spine.

It's a graveyard, a miniature cemetery with five tiny wooden markers close together in a horse-shoe shape, and one larger one set way apart, as if someone didn't want that body buried with the rest.